"You keep surprising me," Wyatt said, picking up a crystal inkwell from the desk. "Just when I think I have you all figured out, you toss something new at me."

Cass smiled faintly. "I've been tempted to throw something at you once or twice since I met you."

He carefully replaced the inkwell. "And I've wrestled with the temptation to shake you . . . or take you to bed." He saw shock widen her eyes, then awareness in their depths as her gaze locked with his. He closed the distance between them in three long strides. Towering over her, he added in a low, quiet voice, "We definitely strike sparks off each other one way or the other. Why do you think that is?"

Her heart raced dangerously fast. She wished he wasn't so close. "It's very simple. You want me to do something I don't want to do."

His smile was soft, his voice low and vibrant. "I think it's more basic than that."

She met his gaze, startled by the deep hunger in his eyes. How could cool blue eyes radiate such heat? she wondered. "No," she protested, denying what she was feeling in hopes of convincing both of them. "I don't want this, Wyatt."

It was the first time she'd said his name. It meant more than she could know, and he'd take whatever small concession she was willing to make. Lowering his head, he decided to find out what else she had to offer him. . . .

WHAT ARE *LOVESWEPT* ROMANCES?

They are stories of true romance and touching emotion. We believe those two very important ingredients are constants in our highly sensual and very believable stories in the *LOVESWEPT* line. Our goal is to give you, the reader, stories of consistently high quality that may sometimes make you laugh, sometimes make you cry, but are always fresh and creative and contain many delightful surprises within their pages.

Most romance fans read an enormous number of books. Those they truly love, they keep. Others may be traded with friends and soon forgotten. We hope that each *LOVESWEPT* romance will be a treasure—a "keeper." We will always try to publish

LOVE STORIES YOU'LL NEVER FORGET
BY AUTHORS YOU'LL ALWAYS REMEMBER

The Editors

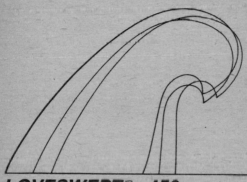

LOVESWEPT® • 452

Patt Bucheister
Tropical Storm

BANTAM BOOKS
NEW YORK • TORONTO • LONDON • SYDNEY • AUCKLAND

TROPICAL STORM

A Bantam Book / February 1991

If you would be interested in receiving protective vinyl
covers for your Loveswept books, please write to this
address for information:

Loveswept
Bantam Books
P. O. Box 985
Hicksville, NY 11802

ISBN 0-553-44076-4

Published simultaneously in the United States and Canada

Bantam Books are published by Bantam Books, a division
of Bantam Doubleday Dell Publishing Group, Inc. Its trademark, consisting of the words "Bantam Books" and the
portrayal of a rooster, is Registered in U.S. Patent and
Trademark Office and in other countries. Marca Regis-
trada. Bantam Books, 666 Fifth Avenue, New York, New
York 10103.

PRINTED IN THE UNITED STATES OF AMERICA

OPM   0 9 8 7 6 5 4 3 2 1

One

Wyatt Brodie tugged at the knot of his tie, hating how constrictive it was. But he had to wear it to get into the exclusive nightclub in Biloxi, Mississippi. There had to be a few things he hated worse than wearing a tie, but at the moment he couldn't think of a single one.

Being strangled by a tie was only one of the sacrifices he was forced to make in order to do a favor for a friend. Nursing a beer for two hours while waiting for an opportunity to talk to a bartender was another. He'd promised to see the woman bartender, not the bulky male one who could easily double as a bouncer—or a Mack truck.

It had taken him two full days to find the woman Delta Crouse wanted him to bring back to Key West. Now that he had, it looked as if he was going to have to wait a little longer before he could talk to her in private.

Leaving Key West was a considerable sacrifice

for a man who preferred to spend his days on or under the sea—and he would leave for only three people. Delta was one of them. The eccentric artist had befriended him, John, and Salem at a time when they badly needed a friend. Now Delta needed a favor, actually two, and Wyatt was determined to do everything in his power to help her. He had to find Delta's daughter and, while he was in the neighborhood, locate Delta's oldest friend, whom she hadn't heard from in two years.

He could only hope this wouldn't take too long. He'd already wasted two days trying to locate Delta's daughter. He'd finally found her, but he wasn't able to talk to her other than to tell her what kind of drink he wanted.

Delta's daughter, he thought, still bemused by the existence of such a person. Going over the details again probably wouldn't help clear up his confusion, but since he didn't have anything else to do at the moment, he gave it a shot.

Cassandra Mason wasn't Delta's niece but her daughter, although she thought she was Delta's niece. The woman Cassandra thought was her mother was actually a friend of Delta's who'd raised her, pretending to be her mother. There had been no mention of Cassandra's father, and Wyatt had been too shocked at the time to ask Delta who he was. Later he didn't ask, for a different reason. If Delta wanted to volunteer the information, fine. If not, that was fine too.

Nope, he thought wearily. It didn't help. The whole jumble of puzzling facts gave him a colossal headache.

That wasn't all that was aching. He shifted his hips, but that brought no relief. The padded leather bar stool might be comfortable for a short period of time, but after perching on it for two hours he felt as if he were sitting on a concrete post. As crowded as the bar was, though, he didn't dare leave the stool to stretch his legs. At least he could watch Cassandra from where he was sitting. It was the closest he'd come to realizing his goal, and he wasn't going to lose his strategic spot now.

His patience was becoming as sore as his rear end, however. Each time he tried to talk to Cassandra Mason, she was called away by one of her demanding customers. He kept waiting for a slack period at the bar, but there didn't seem to be one. Obviously, on a rainy March night in Biloxi, Mississippi, there wasn't much else to do but meet friends at a bar.

After taking another swallow of warm beer, he wondered if she was ever going to take a break. Surely bartenders were allowed coffee breaks or beer breaks, or whatever the hell they were called.

Both Cassandra and the male bartender were kept busy with orders flung at them from waitresses and thirsty customers. The bar was arranged efficiently, saving time and extra steps by having the proper equipment within easy access. It had been built in a U shape with liquor bottles and cash register arranged in the center. Overhead were wooden racks, where glistening stemmed glassware had been shoved into slotted sections. Each time Cassandra needed one of them, she had to stretch her arm up high and stand on her toes. She took care of one side of the bar and the hulking bartender handled the other, and they shared equally the patrons who sat at the bottom of the U.

Since all Wyatt could do for the moment was watch her, he searched for a resemblance between her and Delta. He couldn't see any likeness to the older woman he'd known for fifteen years. Cassandra's hair was a rich auburn compared to Delta's gray-blond; her eyes sea green rather than Delta's pale blue. Even her voice was different, a sultry drawl instead of Delta's matter-of-fact blunt tone. Cassandra's skin was lightly tanned, and he wondered how pale was the skin that hadn't been exposed to the sun.

He couldn't find much left of the shy seventeen-year-old girl who had come to the island ten years before to visit her aunt. Visit the aunt who was actually her mother, he clarified, then stopped himself from going over it all again. No matter how much he mulled on what Delta had told him, he was still unable to understand why she had lied to all of them, and apparently to the girl too.

Cassandra's appearance was the most obvious change he noticed. The tight black vest and ruffled white shirt she wore couldn't completely hide her feminine curves. The uniform certainly looked better on her than on the other bartender. Her black leather skirt came to mid-thigh, exposing a generous expanse of long, shapely legs encased in dark sheer hose. She moved with a lithesome grace that stirred his imagination—and probably every other man's on the long side of fifteen and the short side of eighty.

What was even more surprising was the change in her personality. During the last two hours he had seen her joke with the various customers, mostly men, fending off advances with a smile and a brief remark that didn't offend but still got the message across. She kept a friendly distance between herself and the patrons of the bar with an ease he admired.

Cassandra Mason had definitely grown up.

When she'd taken his drink order two hours earlier, he had noticed her eyes, their expression cool and slightly amused. There hadn't been a flicker of recognition in them, which didn't really surprise him. While she'd been on the island ten years ago, he hadn't seen much of her. When he'd occasionally gone to Delta's for dinner during her brief visit, he had sat at the same table with her, but doubted if they had exchanged more than a few words. He remembered she barely spoke, staring down at her plate while shoving the food around with her fork. Her presence hadn't made much of an impact because she'd remained in the background, even when she was sitting at the table with everyone else. He'd barely noticed when she'd left. She'd never returned. At the time he hadn't wondered why she'd never come back. Now he did.

One of the men down the bar from Wyatt called out to her, "Cass, I need another refill."

"And I need two more hands," she replied with a grin. "Suck on an ice cube for a minute, Jerry. I'll get to you as soon as I can."

It wasn't the first time Wyatt had heard the customers call her Cass instead of the more formal Cassandra. He decided the shortened version of her name suited her better. It was distinctive and unusual. Like her.

His glass was almost empty, but he waited until

she had filled the other orders before catching her eye and lifting his glass.

When she stood in front of him on the other side of the bar, she asked, "Another of the same?"

He nodded. The air was heavy with cigarette smoke and alcohol fumes, but he caught the scent of her, a spicy mixture of exotic perfume and her own special feminine fragrance. Her voice was like honey sliding over dark velvet, creating a frisson of heat through him. This time when he shifted on the bar stool, it had nothing to do with trying to get comfortable. His body reacted before the message eventually reached his brain.

He was attracted to her.

The shy teenager he'd met ten years ago had been negligible, forgotten as soon as she left the room. This woman made his mouth go dry, and his body responded to her cool smile and a smokey voice like a sailor on leave after a long spell at sea.

When she set another frothy glass of beer in front of him, she also set down a small bowl of pretzels. "Maybe you'd better call her," she said gently.

He blinked in surprise. "Call who?"

"The woman you're waiting for."

"What makes you think I'm waiting for a woman?"

She wiped the bar with a clean dry towel. "When a man takes two hours to drink one beer, he isn't here because he's thirsty. It usually means he's waiting for a woman."

"I could be waiting for a man," he said, for the sake of argument.

She shook her head. "You would have left after

the first half hour if you'd been waiting for a man. Only a woman could force a man to wait two hours."

Considering he was waiting to talk to her, he couldn't fault her logic. "You're right. I have been waiting for a woman. Would you believe I've been waiting to talk to you?"

Again she shook her head. "You've been watching me like a scientist examining a specimen in a lab, not like a man who wants to proposition the bartender."

He hadn't realized she'd been aware of his intent gaze. "All I want is to talk to you, not to proposition you."

"You're talking to me."

Placing his forearms on the bar, he leaned toward her, closing the distance between them by a few inches. "I need to talk to you privately. It's important."

She obviously wasn't taking him a bit seriously. "I've heard just about all the approaches there are. Yours needs work."

In an attempt to clear up the wrong impression she had about his motives, he decided to mention Delta's name. Before he could, though, her attention was caught by another patron, and she walked away from him.

Frustration nagged at him. He was never going to be able to talk to her while she was behind the bar. She wasn't taking him any more seriously than she was the other men who made passes at her. He frowned at the thought of her being continually hit on. It didn't help matters to realize he didn't like it. Things were complicated enough without throwing in a physical attraction. Unfortunately it was too late. His body responded to her automatically, like steel filings drawn to a magnet.

When he'd discovered she worked in the bar every night, as well as working for a candy manufacturer Monday through Friday, he had wondered why she worked two jobs. He still didn't know the answer except for the obvious one. Money. Or lack of it. Having worked hard since he was fifteen, he could understand and respect her willingness to support herself, although her current work schedule certainly didn't leave much time for a social life. Even though he worked hard, he made time for play.

When she passed by, he tried again. "Just give me five minutes, Cass. That's all I'll need."

She grinned. "That's what they all say."

He scowled as she continued on her way to tend to another customer down the bar. When he'd first arrived in Biloxi, he'd figured he'd need only a few days to accomplish his errand. He hadn't given much thought to Cass's feelings about going back to Key West. She'd been a means to an end, a way of paying Delta back. Now that he had met Cass, he wanted to find out more about her. She was like the buried treasure he and John sometimes searched for in the Gulf, elusive, mysterious, yet highly desirable. And, at the moment, unattainable.

Cass kept her attention on the drink she was preparing. When the neck of the Scotch bottle clanked a second time against the edge of the glass, she realized her hand was shaking. Even though she wasn't looking directly at him, she could feel the intent gaze of the blond-haired man at the other end of the bar. His constant attention unnerved her, which was strange and vaguely alarming. Lord knows that after two years of working behind a bar, she was accustomed to having men stare at her, but his gaze was different. So was her reaction. Both were unexpected and unwelcome.

The man who had ordered the Scotch grinned at her when she set the glass down in front of him. "Why don't you chuck all this and run away with me tonight, Cassie?"

She took the correct amount of money from the assortment of dollar bills he'd left on the bar. "Because your wife wouldn't like it, Charlie."

Turning to the cash register behind her, she punched in the amount, and her thoughts returned to the man whose eyes followed every move she made. There was something familiar about him, although she was sure he had never been in Chasen's before. She hadn't seen him at Filmer's Fancy Fudge either. Of course tucked away in the art department, she didn't see many people who had business with Filmer's anyway.

Still, the feeling wouldn't go away. She couldn't remember when or where, but she was positive she'd seen him before.

His deeply tanned skin and sun-bleached hair indicated he spent a great deal of time outdoors, but that wasn't much of a clue. It could mean he played golf a lot or worked in construction. He spoke with a slight southern drawl, but so did three-quarters of the residents of Biloxi. No help there either. There was something arresting about him, the way he held himself, as though he was comfortable with his own body, not needing to prove himself to anyone.

She just wished he would stop staring at her with those stunning blue eyes. Slamming the cash register drawer shut, she chanced a look in his direction. She was not at all surprised to meet his gaze. What did surprise her was the way her heartbeat accelerated when her eyes locked with his.

He'd said he wanted to talk to her, and she somehow didn't think it had been a line thrown out as a come-on. She'd heard plenty of them, and his didn't qualify. Whether it was the tone of his voice or his serious expression, she felt he had meant exactly what he said. He wanted to talk to her. But about what? she wondered. And why was she feeling so apprehensive about what he might say?

For a few seconds more she held his gaze, then looked away.

If he was a bill collector, at least he was an attractive one, she mused. She didn't have any outstanding bills at the moment—at least none that she was aware of. Myra's financial affairs had been in such a tangle for so long, though, Cass wouldn't be surprised if he did present her with some new claim.

She discarded that scenario and tried to come up with another one. It would do wonders for her ego if she could believe he was interested in her personally, but that didn't wash either. Giving up, she looked at the slim watch on her wrist. She was due for a break in about fifteen minutes. Just this once she would bend her own rule about never consorting with the customers on her own time.

Wyatt was biting into a pretzel when he felt someone tap him lightly on the shoulder. Turning his head, he saw Cass standing behind him.

Her smile was faint, her voice casual, as she asked, "Do you still want to talk to me?"

Since his mouth was full of pretzel, all he could manage was a nod.

She jerked her head toward the interior of the nightclub. "Come with me, then."

Wyatt followed her, no easy task when he had to weave around solid bodies and tables crammed with people. Instead of looking where he was going, he watched Cass as though she would disappear if he didn't keep her in view. Since she had initiated this meeting, it wasn't likely she would try to elude him, but that didn't stop him from making sure.

Finally she reached an empty booth at the back of the nightclub. "This is about as private as it's going to get." She indicated the small placard in the middle of the table, which read, Reserved. "This booth is for employees to use. I'm going to get something to drink. Would you like anything?"

He shook his head. "Nothing for me, thanks."

He would have liked more privacy, but this was better than nothing and more than he'd thought he would get that night. He'd just come to the conclusion that he might as well go back to his hotel room when she'd tapped him on the shoulder.

As he slid into the booth, he watched her push open a swinging door several feet away and disappear inside. Now that he'd met her, his little rehearsed speech seemed tasteless and blunt. Tact had never been his strong suit, but he was going to need all he could muster now. Since Cass had two jobs, it wasn't going to be easy to convince her to drop everything and return with him to Key West, unless he told her the truth. Finding out that the woman she thought was her aunt was really her mother was going to be an enormous shock. It was Delta's place to explain why she'd kept up the subterfuge for so many years, but he had to get Cass there first.

When Cass returned, she was carrying a glass of milk and a small plate of sugar cookies, which she set down before she slid across the upholstered seat. She leaned back against the booth and looked directly at him, waiting for him to speak. He was silent, though, his intent gaze fixed on her once more.

Determined not to talk first, she picked up her glass and drank from it. Then she picked up a cookie and bit into it. She saw his gaze lower to her mouth. Feeling self-conscious, she licked a crumb off her lips. Sudden heat flared in his eyes.

To get his attention away from her mouth, she pushed the plate of cookies closer to him. "Would you care for one?"

Wyatt shook his head slowly, marveling that the sight of her pink tongue caressing her bottom lip sent shafts of desire through him. Delta's housekeeper would be amazed that he'd turned down a cookie, since he continually raided her cookie jar, but his mind was on other appetites at the moment.

"I've never been in a bar that serves milk and cookies," he said with amusement.

"You still haven't," she answered. "These are my private stash. The cook lets me store them in his kitchen."

"A bartender who drinks milk," he said musingly.

Cass didn't comment. This stranger would think it even more ironic that she worked in a bar if he knew how the abuse of alcohol had affected her life. The one advantage of working behind a bar was that she didn't have to concentrate on what she was doing. Plus, it was one of the few jobs she could work at night.

Wyatt stared as she bit into the cookie again, wondering why he was finding the simple act of eating so arousing. He could tell he was making her uncomfortable, but that was only fair. Simply looking at her was making the fit of his jeans darn painful.

She frowned at him. "Haven't you ever seen anyone eat a cookie before?"

"Not like you do."

She didn't respond to that. "You wanted to talk to me?"

He raised his gaze to meet hers. "Yes." After a brief pause, he added, "You haven't been easy to find."

"I didn't realize I was lost."

"You were for about two years." He smiled when her eyes widened in surprise. "Myra Mason is still misplaced, but I've found Cassandra Mason. One out of two isn't bad."

"What are you?" she asked, caution in her voice and her eyes. "Some kind of detective?"

"Not even close."

The suspense was making her edgy. "You wanted to talk to me, but so far you haven't said much."

"I want you to come to Key West with me. Actually it's Delta Crouse who wants you to come to Key West. She also wanted me to find out why she hasn't heard from her friend in two years. Delta phoned the travel agency Myra owned in New Orleans, only to learn her friend had moved to Biloxi. When I checked the Biloxi phone book, there was no listing of a Mason Travel Agency or Myra Mason, but I did find Cassandra Mason."

Cass stared at him for a long moment, keeping her expression completely blank. Now she knew why she'd felt she had seen him before. She even had a name to go with the face. Wyatt Brodie. Her apprehension tripled when she realized he had been sent by Delta to talk to her. But why?

The only way to find out was to ask. "Why would Delta want me to come to Key West?"

Wyatt noticed she didn't say Aunt Delta, just Delta. "She's very ill. She's asking to see you."

Cass stalled for time by picking up her glass. The milk tasted like cold chalk. Setting the glass back down, she stared at it rather than look at him. "I'm sorry to hear she's been ill. Is it serious?"

"Serious enough. It has something to do with her breathing. She's battled asthma for years, but it's getting worse. She had a bad attack about six months ago and is still recovering. She can't travel, so she asked me to bring you back to the island to see her."

"Why you?"

Wyatt's gaze never left her face. He sensed her withdrawal, although she hadn't moved. "I guess I should have introduced myself. I'm Wyatt Brodie. I met you when you came to the island ten years ago. You also met John Canada and Salem Shepherd. The three of us lived with Delta when we first came to the island."

"I remember. The three orphans Delta took in after you ran away from an orphanage. You and John were learning to dive."

"We have a charter-boat business now. The Gypsy Fleet. John sticks to the fishing charters, and I mostly handle the diving ones. I also have a diving school."

"Do you all still live with Delta?"

"John and Salem were married last year and are expecting their first child soon. They live in a house not far from Delta's. I live in the cottage I used to share with John. Since neither John nor Salem could travel right now because of the baby, Delta asked me to come for you."

Cass smiled faintly. "So you drew the short straw. It's too bad you didn't have my phone number so you could have left a message on my machine. It would have saved you the trip."

This wasn't going very well, Wyatt thought, and he couldn't figure out why. Her reaction wasn't what he'd expected. She was so darned cool rather than seeming even remotely interested. He had no choice but to charge ahead, feeling as ill equipped as a bull who'd had his horns cut off. "It's important that you come back to Key West with me as soon as possible, Cass. I can make the arrangements for a flight out tomorrow. I know that doesn't give you much time, but it's . . ." He stopped reciting his plans when she started to shake her head. "Why not?"

"I have responsibilities, Mr. Brodie. Also two employers who would take a dim view of my giving them an hour's notice that I was leaving. There are other reasons I can't just hop on a plane and take off to Key West. I'm sorry Delta is ill, but I'm neither a nurse nor a particularly close relative. I can't see where I would be much help."

She slid out of the booth and stood up, looking down at him. "She has you and John and Salem, which is the way she wanted it. She made that choice a long time ago."

If he hadn't been so startled by the haunted expression in her eyes, Wyatt might have tried to stop her from walking away. Since he was, all he could do was to sit where she'd left him, stunned by the statement she'd made and the look in her eyes. He watched her return to the bar, her spine straight, her head held high. As he went over what she'd said, he wondered if telling her that Delta was really her mother would make her change her mind. He wasn't so sure. There were undercurrents within undercurrents. It was like diving. He couldn't see the dangerous undertows, only feel them. Something wasn't right.

Because of his promise to Delta, he was determined to convince Cass to change her mind. Earlier he'd thought it would be easy. Now he wasn't sure what it would take.

He remained sitting in the booth rather than return to the bar. He wasn't about to leave without talking to Cass again. From where he sat, he could see her moving back and forth behind the bar as she poured drinks and bantered with the customers. Outwardly she appeared to be the same as before, joking with the customers as though she didn't have a care in the world. But Wyatt could see the way her hand trembled occasionally and the tightening of her lips at odd moments. She didn't look in his direction once.

When the male bartender announced it was closing time, the patrons began to trickle out of the bar. Wyatt was one of the last to leave. Cass was cleaning the remnants of glasses, napkins, and other clutter off the bar as he walked past her. He could see her fingers tighten around the glasses she held, but she didn't speak to him. Nor did he say a word to her.

The cool early-morning air brushed over his heated skin as he stepped outside. The earlier rain had stopped, though the pavement was still wet. It was two in the morning with a full moon overhead. As he walked away from the nightclub, heading around the side for the parking lot, he yanked at the knot of his tie. Once it was loose, he unbuttoned the collar and a couple more buttons down the front of his shirt, then took a deep, welcome breath of the bracing night air. As he rounded the corner of the nightclub, he surveyed the remaining vehicles in the lot. Aside from the rental car he was driving, there were three others. One of them, an older-model compact car, was parked several spaces away from his.

When he reached it, he turned up the collar of his sport coat, crossed his arms over his chest, and leaned his hips against the front left fender.

A half hour later Cass pushed open the back door of the nightclub. Marty usually walked her out to her car, but tonight he had two kegs of beer to install. Rather than wait, she had told him she would be all right getting to her car herself. She was too tired to worry about the possibility of being mugged. Exhaustion lay on her shoulders like a heavy cloak, and her feet were aching—as usual—after an eight-hour stint behind the bar in high-heeled shoes. She slid her hand into one of the side pockets of her black suede jacket, searching for her car keys. All she wanted to do was go home, take a long shower, set her alarm for seven, and fall into bed.

The moment she saw Wyatt Brodie standing beside her car, she knew she wasn't going to get her wish.

She had to use every ounce of self-control to walk toward him without letting him see how tired she was. She didn't want to show any sign of weakness to this man, although for the life of her she didn't know why she felt that way.

She stopped several feet away from him. "How did you know this was my car?"

"Lucky guess," he drawled. "You don't look like the type to drive the pickup or the large van." He gestured to his rental car. "That one's mine, so that leaves this one."

"Very clever deductions, Mr. Brodie. I'm suitably impressed. I'm also very tired. I'd like to go home and get some sleep."

Wyatt could tell she was exhausted by the way she carried herself, and by the mauve shadows of fatigue under her eyes. He was tired, too, and frustrated. He tried to camouflage that frustration, since it was caused more by the situation and the late hour than by her.

"There's one thing," he said, "that I didn't mention earlier. It might make a difference in your decision about going to Key West."

Her fingers clenched painfully around her car keys as she faced him. "Nothing will make a difference, Mr. Brodie. I'm never going back to Key West. If you need it in writing, I'll be glad to oblige. I'll even have it notarized, etched in stone, or carved in wood if it would help you get the message."

"I think what I have to say will make a difference. All you have to do is calm down and listen. It will only take a minute. I promise."

She tried to push him away from her car, but he wouldn't budge. Clamping her fists on her hips, she stepped back and glared at him, then took a deep breath, trying to find some semblance of control over her temper, "Say what you have to say, then, Mr. Brodie, I'm not strong enough to force you to move, and I'm too tired to try."

Feeling as though he were about to drop a rock on a fragile butterfly, he said baldly, "Delta isn't your aunt. She's your mother."

Her answer was quick, brief, and unexpected.

"I know."

Two

Wyatt could only stare at her. The ace he'd played had suddenly turned into a joker. "How long have you known?"

"Ten years. That little tidbit of information was one of the souvenirs I brought back with me when I visited the island."

He leaned against the car. Since Delta wasn't aware Cass knew, the older woman hadn't been the one to tell her. "How did you find out?"

"Does it matter?"

"No, I suppose not." At least not at the moment, he thought. He studied her carefully, trying to see beyond the exhaustion, unable to understand her cool manner. They could have been talking about the weather, for Pete's sake. "You've known all this time, but you haven't been back to see her. Why?"

She smiled thinly. "I could suggest this isn't any of your business, but since she sent you here, I guess in a detached sort of way it is your business. The simple truth is she might have been willing to continue the lie, but I wasn't. Now it doesn't matter." She moved past him to the car door and slipped her key into the lock. "I'm sorry you've been sent on a wild-goose chase, Mr. Brodie. Since I'm the goose you've been chasing, I'd like to point out that your wasted trip isn't my fault."

He pushed away from the car. Reaching out to prevent her from opening the door, he took her hand. "She's ill, Cass. She needs to see you. Give her a chance to explain."

Cass shook her head. "There's nothing to explain. The facts speak for themselves. She didn't want to acknowledge me as her daughter for twenty-seven years. I can't imagine anything she could say that would change that fact." She wrenched open the door, effectively throwing off his hand. "Go back to Key West, Mr. Brodie. You and your two friends will be more comfort to her than I would. She chose to pawn me off on Myra and chose to take you and the other two into her house. She's the one who made the choices, not me."

Cass was relieved when he made no move to try to stop her again. She got in behind the wheel and stuck the key into the ignition, thankful the engine turned over on the first try. As she drove away, she glanced in her rearview mirror and saw Wyatt still standing where she had left him, gazing after her.

She meant what she'd said, although she was afraid it had come out sounding as though she resented him, John, and Salem for being accepted into Delta's home, while she'd been relegated to live with Myra. It hadn't been their fault. She knew it would be difficult, if not impossible, for Wyatt Brodie to understand that she had accepted things the way they were a long time ago. Her life had taught her to depend on only one person, and that was herself.

The following day Cass was able to find an unoccupied park bench in the sun where she could eat her lunch without being disturbed. Because she was taking her lunch hour a little later than usual, most of the other employees of the various firms near the park had returned to their desks.

The sun felt warm and soothing on her skin. One of the drawbacks to working two jobs was she had little time to enjoy the simple pleasures of fresh air and sunshine. Just that morning her boss at Filmer's, Mr. Stanley, had asked when she planned to take her vacation. He'd offered her the use of his condominium in New Orleans, as he did every year for members of his staff. For a few moments she had given herself the luxury of thinking about two weeks without a care in the world other than eating and sleeping. Then she put the tempting thoughts aside. She would be finding a temporary job for her two-week vacation, just as she had for the last couple of years. The financial demands on her didn't take a vacation. They hovered like menacing birds of prey, ready to swoop down and devour her if she didn't keep working.

Closing her eyes, she tilted her face up to catch the rays of the sun, ignoring the sandwich in her lap. How different her life would be if Myra hadn't been injured in the car accident two years ago. Or if Myra hadn't let alcohol take over her life. Or if Myra hadn't accumulated so many debts. At least Myra's health was improving and the financial obligations were finally under control. The previous day, when Cass had visited the clinic where Myra was receiving treatment for her addictions, the nurse in charge had told Cass the doctor was pleased with Myra's progress. Cass had pretended to be enthusiastic, but there had been too many other occasions when improvement had been followed by setbacks.

Maybe if she weren't so tired, she could be more optimistic about Myra's latest treatment. The stress of the last couple of years was beginning to show in subtle ways, and she wasn't sure how much longer she would be able to keep up the pace she'd set for herself.

When she felt a slight movement on the bench next to her, she opened her eyes and turned her head. Seated beside her was Wyatt Brodie.

He was dressed more casually than the previous night, in a pair of tight-fitting jeans and a white shirt worn under a dark blue waist-length zippered jacket. A small logo patch for the Gypsy Fleet was sewn on the left breast pocket. The dark glasses he wore made it impossible for her to see his eyes, but she could feel his gaze aimed at her with the same intensity as the night before.

She probably should have expected to see him again, she mused. She had tried hard not to think of him at all, and had been irritated with herself when thoughts of him kept intruding while she dressed for work, and later while she was bending over her drawing board at Filmer's.

"Hello," he said. His voice was low and cautious, as though he wasn't sure of his reception.

"Hi. You're getting good at this detective business," she murmured. "For someone who works on the sea, you're very efficient on land. How did you find me this time?"

"A small dark-haired girl sitting behind a reception desk at Filmer's Fancy Fudge blabbed where you usually have lunch. Now I know how you've managed to get a tan while working two jobs."

"How did you know where I work?"

"Your neighbor." He hiked one leg over the other, resting his ankle on his knee. "That's a very interesting place you work. I've never seen a purple carpet before."

She told herself she wasn't amused, but it didn't work. His dry sense of humor was only one of the things she found attractive about him. "Mr. Filmer liked purple."

"I saw a large painting of him in the lobby with the dates of his birth and death on a plaque underneath it. Does anyone there realize Mr. Filmer is dead?"

She couldn't help smiling. "There have been rumors to that effect for the last thirty years. I don't know how familiar you are with Filmer's Fancy Fudge, but each box has always been wrapped in purple foil with a single fake gardenia stuck on top. The present administration changed the once-plastic gardenia to the present silk one. I think they wore themselves out making that radical decision and haven't ventured to make another change since."

"What do you do for Filmer's Fancy Fudge?"

"Why don't you ask my neighbor? She seems to

have been a regular fountain of information so far."

"More like a flash flood," Wyatt muttered, remembering how difficult it had been to get away from the woman. "Except she didn't know exactly what your line of work was."

"Well, even the best detectives run into problems once in a while. Just to save you a little time, and since it's no major secret, I'll help you out. I work in the art department. We do advertisements for magazine layouts and two catalogs a year."

"I bet you use a lot of purple," he said dryly.

To the point where she thought she would throw up sometimes if she had to look at that shade of deep purple ever again, she admitted to herself.

"Why do you work at a job you don't like?" he asked, apparently reading her mind.

Rather than admit he was right, she countered with a question of her own. "What makes you think I don't like my job?"

"When we first arrived in Key West, John took the first job he could find to bring in some money. It was cleaning fish. When he came in every night, he had a look in his eyes that had nothing to do with the smell of fish clinging to his clothes and his skin. You had the same expression in your eyes just now."

His perception scared her in a deep, primitive way, as though he could see into her soul. "John did what he had to do," she said flatly. "That's what I'm doing." Changing the subject, she asked, "Have you had lunch?"

"No," he answered cautiously. "Why?"

She lifted the sandwich from her lap and held it out to him. "How do you feel about chicken salad?"

"Impartial," he said, smiling. "You eat it. It's your lunch."

Shaking her head, she dropped it back on her lap. "I've suddenly lost my appetite." She tilted her head to one side as she looked at him. "You're very persistent. I have to give you that. I don't know what more I can do to try to convince you I meant what I said last night. I'm not going back to Key West with you."

He stretched his long legs out in front of him, leaning back against the hard bench. "One thing you might as well know about me, Cass. I'm not only persistent, I'm stubborn. To give you an example, it took us over two years to locate a sunken ship we were hired to find. We didn't give up then, and we had the benefit of a chart. With you I'm sailing blind, but I'm not giving up."

She shrugged. "I hope you've found a comfortable place to stay in Biloxi, Mr. Brodie. You're going to be here for a long time."

For several moments he simply looked at her. "You don't like talking about yourself, do you?" he said abruptly. "If it's because you don't think you're an interesting topic of conversation, you're wrong."

"Oh, I think I'm interesting," she said, giving him a mocking smile. "I just don't expect other people to think so. Nor do I particularly care."

"Maybe if you gave them something to go on . . ." he said softly, then stopped and went down a different track. "I don't understand you. You have a chance to know your real mother, and you aren't taking it."

"I know my mother, Mr. Brodie. She's the woman who raised me, who patched my skinned knees, helped me with my homework, and stayed up nights when I was sick. Her name is Myra Mason."

He didn't debate the point. "Delta's been concerned about her too. Apparently it's been a long time since Mrs. Mason has written or called Delta."

"Miss."

"What?"

"It's Miss Mason. Myra never married."

And, Wyatt mused, the man who fathered Cass never married Delta. These women didn't seem to want any men in their lives, and he wondered if Cass felt the same way.

Instead of asking her, he concentrated on Myra. "Where is Miss Mason now?"

Cass looked away, staring off into the distance. "She's been recovering from injuries sustained in a car accident." It was the stock answer she always gave.

"Why didn't you let Delta know? She's been worried about both of you."

"Frankly it never occurred to me to notify her."

Wyatt removed his sunglasses in order to see her better. The color of her suit had appeared a dull gray through the dark lenses of his glasses. Now he could see it was a soft pearly shade that went well with her plain white blouse. She wore less makeup than she had the previous night, leaving her skin fresh and touchable.

Realizing how badly he wanted to stroke her

skin, he yanked his attention back to the original subject before he did something incredibly stupid. Like pushing her down on the park bench and discovering how she tasted.

"You have a right to be bitter because Delta ignored you all these years, but she's at least trying to make up for it now. I think you should give her a chance."

"And I think you don't know what you're talking about." She gathered up her sandwich and purse, then stood up. "I have to be getting back to work, Mr. Brodie. I'd like to tell you to stay away from me, but I doubt if you would pay any attention. You've ignored everything else I've told you so far." She waved her free hand in a gesture that signified she didn't care one way or the other. "You do what you have to do. Just don't be too surprised when none of it works."

He sprang off the bench and grabbed her arm as she started to walk away. Pulling her around, he brought her up close to him, his gaze hard and determined as he looked down at her. "I'm not buying any of this."

"Good," she said defiantly, wishing he hadn't touched her. "Because I'm not selling anything."

"Yes, you are. You're trying to sell me on the impression that you're one tough cookie, a real hard-boiled egg. The woman who gave birth to you is seriously ill, and you pretend you couldn't care less. I think you care, but you'll be damned if you'll admit it. If this is your idea of revenge for the way she treated you, green eyes, it's lousy timing."

The sun was in her eyes, but that wasn't the only reason she briefly closed them. She needed to shut out the expression on his face, but she still saw the male arousal and challenge in his eyes. His body was only inches away from hers; his touch created a riot of sensations deep inside her. She didn't need this, she told herself fiercely. She didn't want to be attracted to him. And she might as well wish for the moon to rise at noon for all the good it was doing, trying to talk herself out of it.

She opened her eyes. "Whether I care or not doesn't change anything. I can't go to Key West."

She broke from his tight hold and quickly walked away. Wyatt didn't go after her, his eyes narrowed as he watched her. The last thing she said ran through his mind several times. She had said she *can't* go to Key West, not that she didn't want to go. That implied there were reasons other than her simply not wanting to face Delta. The most obvious one was that she couldn't afford to take time away from her two jobs.

Somehow he was going to have to find out more information about Miss Cassandra Mason, which wasn't going to be easy. Ever since he'd arrived in Biloxi, he'd run into one brick wall after another. If it wasn't for the chatty neighbor who'd happened to pass by when he'd been pounding on Cass's front door that morning, he would never have known where she worked. The neighbor had been no help, however, when he'd asked about Myra Mason. Cass had told him Myra had been in a car accident, but she hadn't said how extensive the older woman's injuries were, or where she was now. He kept getting so sidetracked when he was with Cass, he continually forgot he had two missions to accomplish.

His priority now was to find out why she needed to work two jobs so that he could figure out how much money she needed to tide her over while she was in Key West. He didn't care how much it cost him. He was going to keep his promise to Delta if it took every penny he had.

Cass had been working at the bar for three hours when she felt a prickly sensation at the base of her neck. Jerking her head around, she scanned the faces of the occupants of the bar stools, looking for a blond-haired man with piercing blue eyes. Wyatt wasn't among the patrons at the bar, but that didn't mean he wasn't sitting in one of the booths or at a table out of her view.

An hour later Marty, the other bartender, came off his break. Cass was wiping her hands on a towel, and she almost dropped it when Marty told her how he'd spent his break.

"That guy you took your break with last night is either planning to write your life history or he's got it bad. I haven't had so many questions fired at me about a woman I work with since my ex-wife's lawyer had me in court."

So she'd been right, Cass thought with satisfaction. Wyatt was there. "What kind of questions did he ask?"

Marty grinned. "Sorry. It's classified material."

"Not if it's about me."

Shrugging, Marty skirted the issue by saying, "When I left, he'd corralled Cynara and was chatting her up."

Cass looked down and saw she'd viciously twisted the towel she was holding. Too bad it wasn't Wyatt Brodie's neck, she thought as she flung the towel onto the bar. "Where is he?" she asked in a low, furious voice.

"Second booth from the back, your side of the bar. Don't worry, Cass. No one will tell a stranger anything about you, even if we knew anything to tell."

"That's not what I'm concerned about."

One of her customers raised his hand to indicate he needed a drink. Marty gave her a gentle shove toward the hinged flap on the counter that they used to exit the bar. "I'll take care of your orders. Go talk to him. If you need me, whistle, and I'll be there."

When Cass reached the booth where Wyatt was supposed to be, she found it empty. Glancing around, she glimpsed Cynara pushing open the door to the kitchen and followed her. Apparently still on her break, Cynara was helping herself to some french fries from the heating rack.

"Can I talk to you a few minutes, Cynara?" Cass asked.

"Sure. Want some fries?"

"No, thanks." Cass leaned on the stainless steel counter next to Cynara. "Marty said you were talking to a blond man who was asking a lot of questions about me."

Cynara reached for a bottle of ketchup and upended it over the fries. "Good-looking guy too. I'd hoped he was interested in me when he approached me, but as luck would have it, all he wanted to do was ask me questions about you."

"Like what?"

"Like how long have you worked here? When's your day off? He even wanted to know the manager's name. What's going on, Cass? Why doesn't he find out all this stuff from you?"

Taking one of the french fries off Cynara's plate, Cass said, "He's shy."

Cynara nearly choked on the fry she had bitten into. After Cass patted her between the shoulders several times, she cleared her throat and said, "If he's shy, I'm Princess Di."

"What he is is a pain in the neck," Cass grumbled.

"He's a man, Cassie. I haven't seen a man yet who isn't a pain somewhere. It goes with the territory. But when they fill out a pair of tight jeans like he does, it helps ease the pain. You know what I mean?"

Unfortunately she did. Without commenting, Cass stole another fry off Cynara's plate and walked over to the refrigerator to pour herself a glass of milk. Victor, the cook, shooed her away with a flow of incomprehensible Italian, as he did every night. Since he always smiled and blew her a kiss before she left, she never took offense.

After her break was over, she returned to the bar without catching a glimpse of Wyatt. Twice she was reminded he was still there. One of the regulars told her he'd just had a drink with her boyfriend, and another of the waitresses winked at her, congratulating her on finding such a hunk.

If she ever did find him, Cass thought, she was going to wring his neck, then shove him on a plane for Key West. The man had nerve, she had to give him that.

He also managed to stay invisible, at least to her, the rest of the evening. When she left the club after it closed, she half-expected to see him waiting for her at her car, as he had the previous night. He wasn't there. She had a hard time convincing herself that what she was feeling wasn't disappointment.

As she drove home, she tried to figure out what kind of game he was playing now. The night before he'd stuck to her like gum on the bottom of her shoe, impossible to get rid of and irritating as hell. He'd even come to the park while she was having lunch. Then tonight he chatted with everyone in the bar except her.

She nearly missed a red traffic light and had to slam on the brakes. She tightened her grip on the wheel and took a deep, steadying breath. The man was driving her crazy, certifiably bonkers. Whether he was with her or not, he was capable of turning her into a blithering idiot. She didn't need this. She had plenty of problems without a new one named Wyatt Brodie.

Her latest problem was waiting for her on her doorstep.

Wyatt was sitting on the steps leading up to the front door of the apartment complex. He stood up as she approached, his movements slower than normal. He obviously wasn't too spry at three in the morning.

Cass weighed her options, the first one being to throw her shoes at him. Another was to throw herself into his arms, but she quickly discarded that. There was always the police, but since the only threat Wyatt Brodie posed was to her sanity and not her health, she doubted they'd do her much good. She chose her last option.

"You might as well come in," she said, "so I can

tell you for the hundredth time that I won't be going back to Key West with you."

"It's what I live for."

He fell in beside her as she crossed the small lobby and punched the button to summon the elevator. "I wouldn't turn down a cup of coffee," he added.

"I don't have any coffee," she said through clenched teeth. "I don't drink coffee."

The doors to the elevator opened, and he followed her inside. "Not even in the morning?"

He sounded downright shocked. She glanced at him. He looked shocked. She punched the button for the third floor, fighting a smile. "Not even in the morning. I have a glass of milk instead."

He shuddered. "We might not get along after all."

Cass brushed past him when the elevator doors opened. "I could have told you that yesterday."

He shortened his stride in order to walk beside her. "There's a saying about opposites attracting."

"I don't think a law of physics applies here." She shoved her key into the lock, then turned the knob when it clicked open. "I can't guarantee I'll stay awake long, Mr. Brodie, so I hope you've prepared a brief statement. Anything longer than five minutes, and I'll be asleep."

"I'll find some way of keeping you awake," he said softly, his gaze holding hers for a long moment.

Pushing open the door, Cass muttered something under her breath and entered her apartment.

Chuckling, Wyatt followed her in.

She walked over to a small table and turned on the lamp sitting on top of it. "Which reminds me. Where do you get off talking to the people I work with and the customers in the club? You have no right asking them questions about me."

He removed her keys from the door and shut it behind him. "I talked to them because your life is not exactly an open book. I decided to turn a few pages." He dropped the keys on the table. "That's all."

She kicked off her shoes and sank down onto the sofa, closing her eyes as the cushions absorbed her weight. "This is a private edition, not for public display."

When a minute went by without him speaking, she opened her eyes and saw him glancing around the room. The light from the single lamp did not show off the furnishings at their best. But then, to see the furniture at its best would mean going back forty years to when it was new. Each piece was a well-loved and well-worn item chosen by Myra over the years, and Cass had salvaged some of the furniture when Myra's accident had forced her to give up her expensive apartment in New Orleans. And her job with an advertising agency.

Wyatt looked at her. "Are you sure you're Cassandra Mason?"

For some reason she found his question funny rather than absurd. Grinning at him, she replied, "If I'm not, I have her driver's license."

His fleeting smile acknowledged her point. "I might not score high on a test for Einstein's assistant, but I'm reasonably good at remembering what I'm told. Most of the information I was given on Myra and Cassandra Mason has had to be tossed. You both were supposed to be in New Orleans. Instead you're in Biloxi, Mississippi. There's no travel agency, no apartment in the French Quarter, no job at a prestigious ad agency. Instead you have a job you obviously dislike and tend bar. You can't blame me for being curious."

"I also don't have to explain how I live my life to you or anyone else."

"You don't have to, but it would certainly make a nice change," he murmured as he tore his gaze from her to scan the bare walls. "Where are your paintings?"

She frowned. He shifted gears faster than a race driver. "What paintings?"

"Delta said you showed extraordinary talent as an artist when you were on the island. She said you used to spend most of your time in her studio painting. She was very proud that you'd inherited her talent."

Cass looked away. When she'd returned from Key West that summer, she had thrown out her brushes, her paints, and her dream about becoming an artist. That dream had been destroyed when she'd overheard Delta tell her housekeeper that she'd done the right thing by giving Cass to her friend to raise, so that Delta could pursue her art. Life was full of compromises, and Cass's had been to use her artistic ability to design only what a client wanted, never giving in to the desire to express herself on canvas. Painting had been Delta's main focus in life, to the exclusion of everything else, including her own child. Cass wasn't about to let it take over her own life.

She hadn't told Myra or anyone what she'd

heard that summer in Key West. She certainly wasn't about to tell Wyatt Brodie.

"Delta was wrong," she said. "I didn't inherit anything from her."

Wyatt picked up a crystal inkwell from the set on the small oak desk. "You keep surprising me. Just when I think I have you all figured out, you toss something new at me."

She smiled. "I've been tempted to *throw* something at you once or twice since I met you."

He carefully placed the inkwell back in its place. "And I've wrestled with the temptation either to shake you until your teeth rattle or to take you to bed." He saw shock widen her eyes, then awareness flare in their depths as her gaze locked with his. He closed the distance between them in three long strides. Towering over her, he added in a low, quiet voice, "We definitely strike sparks off each other, one way or the other. Why do you think that is?"

Her heart started to beat dangerously fast. She wished he wasn't so close. "It's very simple. You want me to do something I don't want to do."

His smile was tender, his voice vibrant. "I think it's more basic than that."

She held his gaze, startled by the deep hunger in his eyes. How could cool blue eyes radiate such heat? she wondered abstractedly. Were her own eyes revealing her reaction as obviously as his were?

"No," she protested, denying what she was feeling in the hope of convincing both of them.

To put necessary distance between them, she pushed herself off the sofa and started to move away. She had taken two steps when his hand closed over her arm, stopping her. Another theory, the one about every action causing a reaction, was proven true when Wyatt applied pressure on her arm at the same time she tried to pull away. If she had had any breath left, it would have been knocked out of her by the impact of her smaller frame against his solid body.

"I don't want this, Wyatt," she said, gasping for air.

It was the first time she'd used his given name. It meant more to him than it would have with anyone else. With her he would take whatever small concession she was willing to make. Lowering his head, he decided to find out what else she had to offer him.

Her lips were parted slightly when he covered her mouth with his, allowing him access to her warmth. His hands at her waist tightened, and he deepened the kiss. The air splintered around him as her mouth opened on a sigh, drawing him down into the dark, beckoning realm of passion. His arms went around her to keep her locked to him, her softness pressed against him.

When he raised his head to look down at her, he thought he would explode with need as she stroked her bottom lip with her tongue, as though relishing the taste of him. She was the most naturally sensual woman he'd ever met, and he wanted her with a wild hunger he'd never experienced before.

Despite the demands of his body screaming out for release, he gently pushed her away from him. "Cass," he murmured, "we need to talk."

For a moment Cass simply looked at him, her lips throbbing from his kiss. The desire he had stroked to life with his lips spun through her. She nodded briefly and backed away from him, crossing her arms over her middle in a defensive gesture.

"Cass, tell me how much money you need," he said gruffly. "We'll go on from there."

All the color drained from her face. The hot passion he had stoked into flames instantly turned to cold ashes. Before she realized what she was doing, she flung out her hand and struck him across the face.

"I'm not some whore you picked up on a street corner, Mr. Brodie. Get the hell out of my apartment and my life."

Three

Stunned, Wyatt raised his hand to his jaw. He didn't know which shocked him more, what she'd done or what she'd said.

"I didn't mean what you think, Cass," he said quietly, lowering his hand. "I want to know how much money you'll need to replace the wages you'll be losing when you come to Key West."

She shook her head in exasperation. "You've been spending too much time underwater. It's affected your hearing. How many times do I have to tell you I'm not going to Key West before you'll believe me?"

"You can say it as many times as you want if it makes you feel any better," he murmured dryly. "But you're still going."

Cass tightened her arms around her waist, trying to contain the trembling deep inside her. He sounded so sure of himself, she was beginning to believe she was actually going to do as he said. Still reeling from the few minutes she had spent in his arms, she felt the sensual pull toward him and fought it for all she was worth. Even though she was too tired to resist him or the attraction, she knew she had to.

Wyatt saw her sway slightly and closed the distance between them. Taking her arm, he led her over to the couch and gently forced her to sit down before she fell down. He knew he was being unfair to push the issue home when she was so tired, but he was running out of time.

Her eyes closed as she laid her head against the back of the couch, her arms still wrapped around herself. He was mesmerized by the sight of her long lashes resting on her cheeks.

"Do you have to work tomorrow?" he asked.

She didn't open her eyes. "What's tomorrow?"

It was already tomorrow, but he didn't quibble. "Saturday."

"I have the weekend off from Filmer's. I have my usual shift at the bar."

Resisting the temptation to run his finger over the pale, soft skin where her lashes lay, he turned away from her and went in search of the kitchen. It wasn't difficult to find, since the apartment consisted of only three rooms. Other than the living room and the kitchen, one door led off the narrow hallway to, he guessed, the bedroom and bathroom.

Thinking about her stretched out on her bed didn't help his control. It wouldn't take much for him to give in to the desire seething under his skin. He remembered her response, brief though it had been, when he'd kissed her. It had been enough to make him want to continue exploring her mouth, and then the rest of her body. But the timing was wrong. She was tired, angry, and vulnerable. When he made love to her, he wanted her wide awake and fully aware of what she was doing and what he was doing to her. And the time would come, he promised himself.

When he stopped in front of the refrigerator, he had to unclench his hand in order to open the door. As he glanced inside, he decided her refrigerator made Old Mother Hubbard's cupboard look overstocked. All it contained was a gallon of milk, a carton of eggs, and four cans of strawberry soda. He grimaced at the thought of drinking the sweet strawberry drink at that hour of the morning, or any other time for that matter.

At least she wouldn't have to be concerned about any food spoiling while she was gone, he thought ruefully. And she was going if he had to carry her kicking and screaming onto the airplane.

He set the milk container on the counter and found a glass in the first cupboard he opened. He would have given all the cash in his wallet for a steaming cup of strong coffee, but she at least would be satisfied with milk.

He carried the full glass into the living room, his gaze automatically fixing on her. Her eyes were still closed, her breathing slow and deep as she lay on her side on the flowered cushions. One of her small hands was lying beside her face, the fingers curled slightly in a defenseless pose.

He never took his eyes off her as he went down on his haunches to study her. He debated waking her. They still had a few things to settle. When he lifted his free hand toward her shoulder, she sighed heavily in her sleep, her lips parting slightly. He withdrew his hand.

He set the glass on the coffee table, then lifted her legs up onto the sofa. He kept his movements slow and gentle so that he wouldn't wake her, although he was beginning to think nothing short of a bomb would rouse her from her deep sleep. She would be more comfortable in her own bed, and out of the leather skirt and snug vest, but that would require more self-control than he trusted himself to provide. He settled for unfastening several buttons of her shirt, stopping when he caught a glimpse of delicate white lace underneath. Easing her black heels off her feet demanded more concentration than it should have, mainly because his hands weren't as steady as he would have liked.

For a long moment he simply watched her as she slept, fascination keeping him there when he should have left so that he, too, could get some badly needed sleep. He stared at her as though the answers to some puzzling questions could be found in her features. He wasn't as surprised to feel sexually attracted to her as he was to feel such a strange, strong need to protect her, to keep her safe.

His mouth twisted as he realized he was the only one threatening her peace of mind at the moment.

The stiffness in his legs reminded him he'd been in the same position for a long time. He took the glass of milk back to the kitchen and left it in the refrigerator. Returning to the living room, he stared down at her for several minutes before turning off the lamp—after he picked up her key ring from the table.

Cass closed her eyes as she tilted her head back to let the water spray directly on her face. Since the water pressure in her shower had always been more like a gentle summer rain, the spray didn't hurt at all. But the warm water sluicing over her skin helped to clear her mind and to ease muscles cramped from spending what remained of the night on her couch.

Thank heavens it was Saturday, she thought for the third time since she'd opened her eyes. She'd managed to sleep for five delicious hours, even if it was on her short couch and while she was still dressed. Sleep was sleep, no matter how she managed to get it.

Smiling at the thought of how her falling asleep had gotten rid of Wyatt Brodie better than anything she had ever said to him, she turned off the water. Her smile vanished as she reached for a towel. He would be back. She knew that as well as she knew the sun would rise each morning and set each night.

After shrugging on her kimono-style robe, she wiped the steam off the mirror above the sink and looked at her reflection. Bringing her hand up to her mouth, she ran her forefinger across her bottom lip, remembering the feel of his firm mouth covering hers. She had been kissed before, occasionally when she hadn't wanted to be kissed by a man who expected a reward at the end of a rare evening out. Other times she had welcomed the sign of affection. But never before had she ever felt the tangle of emotions Wyatt had caused when he kissed her.

In such a short time he had complicated her life by his demands, his presence, creating strange yearnings deep within her.

As she stared at her reflection, she came to a decision. She would go to Key West after all. It was time to confront the past. Always honest with herself, she knew that though she'd accepted her circumstances, an underlying resentment against them always dwelt within her. Feeling rejected by her own mother had left a scar that needed to be eradicated if she was ever going to heal. It had affected every relationship in her life, even with Myra.

If she was going to learn to trust anyone, she was going to have to see Delta, get to know her better, find out what kind of woman could abandon her own child. Accepting the past was one thing. She wanted to understand the person who had been forever in the background of her life like a dark shadow.

She also admitted to herself that Wyatt Brodie had something to do with her decision. She needed to understand why he affected her the way he did, to explore the sensations he stirred within her.

Plus, she badly needed a rest. For two years she'd been pushing herself to the limit, getting very little sleep, even less relaxation or fun. She hated her job at Filmer's; tending bar was a test of her stamina; and she wasn't sure how much longer she would be able to go on with either one.

Myra's therapy depended on counselors at this stage. The older woman was getting the best of care and could be left for two weeks without any problems. As part of the therapy, Myra wasn't allowed visitors at this point, so she needn't even be aware Cass was gone.

Financially it wasn't a wise decision to make, but she could always make up for the loss of income when she returned. The payments to the clinic were up to date, and she had enough set aside for the first-of-the-month expenses. The last two years would have been much easier if Myra hadn't neglected to make her health insurance payments, which had resulted in her coverage being canceled.

She had a two-week paid vacation she could take from Filmer's, but none from the bar. She smiled at her reflection. She hadn't done anything really stupid for a long time. She was due.

Tightening the belt at her waist, she opened the bathroom door. She'd taken two steps into her bedroom when she stopped abruptly. Her suitcase was open on her bed. As she walked slowly toward it, she saw that some of her clothes were piled haphazardly on each side of the open case. If a burglar had packed it, he or she hadn't been concerned with neatness.

Then she heard a noise coming from her kitchen. She paused to try to determine what had made the sound. Then she heard it again. It sounded as if someone was juggling with her pots and pans.

She stepped over to the open door of her bedroom. She smelled coffee. And bacon.

Retreating back into her bedroom, she walked over to the closet and took out the baseball bat she kept on hand for protection. If it was a burglar, he had chosen a rather poor pigeon to pluck.

She didn't have much experience with the way burglars worked, but she thought it was odd he would bring his own coffee and proceed to cook himself a meal. Which left someone who wasn't a burglar or particularly shy about making himself at home. Wyatt Brodie. The baseball bat was in case she was wrong.

Her bare feet made no sound on the wooden floor as she crept down the hallway to the kitchen. Holding the bat tightly in her hands, she rounded the corner and stopped in the doorway.

Wyatt stood at the stove turning strips of bacon in a frying pan. A blue chambray shirt was tucked into his jeans, the sleeves rolled up several turns on his forearms. He looked up and saw her armed with a baseball bat. His eyes sparkled with amusement.

"Good morning," he said casually. His gaze flowed over her, from her feet, up her bare legs, over the skimpy robe, to her face. His expression indicated he appreciated what he saw. A brow lifted as his glance slid again to the bat. "If you plan on playing some ball this morning, you're not exactly dressed for it."

She lowered the bat, resting it on her shoulder. "What are you doing?" she asked as she leaned against the door frame.

He flipped over another slice of bacon. "I think that's rather obvious. I'm making breakfast."

"I can see that. Do you make a habit of breaking into people's homes to cook breakfast?"

"I didn't break in."

"Would it do me any good to ask how you did get in?"

"I used your key. How do you like your eggs?"

"Poached."

He gave her a pained look. "Sorry. That's out of my league. I can do sunny-side up, scrambled, or overcooked. Take your pick."

Pushing away from the door frame, she set the bat down against the wall. "Call me foolish, but I have a feeling you will make them exactly the way you want no matter what I say." Taking in the carton of eggs, the half-empty package of bacon, and the large Styrofoam container of coffee on the counter, she murmured, "You've been busy this morning."

He shrugged as he speared another strip of bacon and turned it over. "I was hungry, and I figured you could use a good breakfast too."

Cass didn't bother informing him she rarely ate breakfast. Instead she stepped around him so that she could open the refrigerator door. The first thing she noticed was the glass of milk sitting on the top shelf. She didn't ask him when he'd poured it. She was discovering that when confronted by an unmovable object, it was easier to go around it rather than knock her head against it. Leaning her hip against the counter, she calmly sipped her milk and watched him cook.

Wyatt wasn't sure whether he'd won or lost this round. The calm way Cass had accepted his presence in her apartment unnerved him. He hadn't been as surprised to see her wielding the baseball bat as by her putting it down without using it. When he'd taken her keys last night, it had been a purely impulsive action. Knowing how tired she was, he hadn't planned on arriving at her door quite this early, but after receiving a phone call from Salem, he had moved his schedule up several hours.

Her voice broke into his thoughts. "I didn't realize you knew how to cook."

"That sounds like a sexist remark."

"Not really. I'm just surprised you ever learned. I remember the housekeeper being possessive of her kitchen. I don't imagine that changed. I find it difficult to picture Connie letting you near her stove."

He chuckled. "She didn't. John and I lived on our own for a long time before he got married. When we got sick of peanut butter sandwiches and frozen dinners, we decided to tackle cooking or starve."

"I thought you and John ate all your meals at Delta's. You did when I was there ten years ago."

"Not all the time. We have weekend cruises when we need to provide food for our clients, plus we didn't always get back into port by dinnertime." His gaze narrowed as he studied her closely. "Does that bother you? That we've been treated like family even though we aren't related to Delta?"

She shook her head. "I learned a long time ago not to regret something I can't change or control."

He continued to watch her. She had placed her free hand on the counter, and the front of the robe had parted just enough to give him a tantalizing view of satiny skin and the gentle slope of one of her breasts. Good Lord, he thought. She didn't have a damn thing on under that poor excuse for a robe.

Tearing his gaze away from her, he said quietly,

"Your mother took a turn for the worse during the night."

She had been about to take another sip of milk, but her hand froze at his words. As she stared at him, she wondered how he knew that. She hadn't heard the phone ring, and she'd received enough late-night and early-morning emergency phone calls during the last two years, that she always woke at the first ring. Perhaps the call had come while she was in the shower. But how he knew didn't matter. What he knew did.

Setting the glass down on the counter, she stood up straight, as though readying herself for the worst. "Is she still at the clinic or did they take her to the hospital?"

"Clinic?" he asked, his voice registering his confusion. "She's not in any clinic. She's at home."

Cass closed her eyes briefly as she leaned back against the counter for support. She took a deep breath and opened her eyes to meet his concerned gaze. "I didn't realize you meant Delta. I thought something had happened to Myra."

"I said your mother had a turn for the worse. Delta is your mother."

"Don't start that again," she said wearily. She picked up her glass and sat down at the table. "How is Delta?"

"Salem phoned me at the hotel early this morning," he said as he lay the cooked bacon on a plate and reached for the carton of eggs. "Delta had difficulty breathing during the night. She refused to go to the hospital, so Connie called her nephew, who's the doctor taking care of her. He came out to the house and put her on oxygen."

He paused, then added, "We might be running out of time, Cass."

She watched a drop of moisture slowly run down the side of her glass, growing in size and sliding faster until it fell onto the table. She felt her problems were like that drop of moisture, gaining momentum and size and racing out of control.

Suddenly a piece of paper was placed on the table in front of her. She picked it up. It was a blank personal check made out to her. Wyatt had signed it. "What's this for?"

"Put in whatever amount you need to cover your expenses while you're gone."

"This isn't necessary."

"Apparently money is a problem or you wouldn't be working two jobs and living in a dinky apartment."

He'd returned to the stove by the time she'd folded the check and slipped it into her pocket. She was never going to cash it, but he didn't have to know that right now. She wasn't up to arguing about it.

She looked at him as he cracked eggs into the frying pan. "What time is the flight to Key West?"

His head jerked around and he stared at her. The egg he'd just cracked oozed out of the shell and plopped into the pan, but he didn't even notice. "You're going?"

Her smile was faint, her voice resigned. "I need to make some phone calls and a few arrangements. Then I can leave." She repeated her earlier question. "What time is the flight?"

Wyatt's eyes narrowed. Now that she'd agreed, he had to wonder why. It had been too easy after all the strong protests she'd made the last couple of days. Apparently his check made the difference.

He answered her question. "Four o'clock." Then he asked one of his own. "Why, Cass? Why are you finally agreeing to go?"

She stood up and pushed her chair in, then carried the glass to the sink and rinsed it out. "You win, I'm going to Key West. Why question it?"

Undeterred, he asked again, "Why are you agreeing to go with me?"

"It must be your persuasive nature."

He muttered a succinct two-syllable curse.

"Probably," she said dryly, as though the blunt word required a reply. "That describes your line of persuasion nicely. Now, if you'll excuse me, I've got some packing to do. Not that I don't appreciate your already starting the process, but I think I'll do that part myself, if you don't mind."

The smell of burning food jerked his attention back to the frying pan. A few more colorful curses escaped his lips as he scooped up the crisp fried eggs with a spatula and threw them down the garbage disposal. When he turned around to ask Cass again why she'd changed her mind, she had left the kitchen.

Picking up a strip of bacon, he bit into it as he thought about the last ten minutes. Her cool acceptance bothered him. He'd only known her for two days, so he probably wasn't the best one to judge whether or not Cassandra Mason was prone to changing her mind quickly. He didn't think so, however. She was obviously willing to work for whatever money she needed, yet she had taken his check.

For as long as he could remember, he had trusted his instincts and had found them to be fairly accurate. He'd instinctively trusted John and Salem years ago, a trust that had never been betrayed. Underwater he used his instincts as well as his extensive training, and had found one as important as the other.

Right now his instincts were screaming at him that there was more behind Cass's agreement to come to Key West than she was giving away. He didn't know why he was harping on the fact that she'd changed her mind. She was going to Key West with him. It was what he wanted, the reason he'd come to Biloxi looking for her.

So why was he suddenly apprehensive about taking her to Key West?

After she dried her hair, it took Cass only a few minutes to slip into a pair of white linen slacks and a light blue cotton sweater before she tackled the job of packing enough clothes for two weeks. The years of traveling when Myra had owned the travel agency paid off now as she sorted through the clothes in her closet and bureau drawers. Myra's advice had always been to pack for the weather conditions, to keep in mind the location and what type of activities she would be involved in, and always to remember that less is more. The sign of an inexperienced traveler was packing every item in one's closet.

She picked out cool clothing, mostly shorts and lightweight shirts and skirts. She added several pairs of sandals and included a dress and a pair of heels, even though she wasn't expecting to go out; it was as automatic as packing her toothbrush and hair dryer.

As she snapped the locks on the packed suitcase, Wyatt spoke behind her. "Breakfast is ready."

"I'm really not hungry, Wyatt," she said, lifting the suitcase off the bed. "Why don't you go ahead and eat?"

"You should eat something." He glanced down at the suitcase, then met her gaze. "Is this all you're taking?"

She smiled. "I'm not going to be there all that long."

He pressed his back against the door frame as she brushed past him on her way to the living room. By the time he caught up with her, she was leafing through a small notebook that had been under the phone. He stopped her from picking up the receiver by grabbing her wrist. "What do you mean you're not going to be in Key West long?"

She removed his hand. "I can only take two weeks from my job at Filmer's," she said firmly, her gaze on the phone as she stabbed out a series of numbers.

Two weeks, he speculated. It wasn't all that long, but it was better than nothing. He should be glad she was coming to the island at all.

He realized she was phoning her boss at his home when he heard her explaining that a family emergency required her to take her two-week vacation right away. Apparently her employer didn't like the short notice, but Cass was adamant. Her voice was quiet and calm, her manner businesslike and formal as she gave detailed explanations about who should deal with her work and how.

Next she phoned the bar manager, also at his home. She sat down on the couch, settling the phone on one of her thighs as she again explained she wouldn't be in to work for the next two weeks. At one point Wyatt saw a frown appear between her brows, but her voice remained even and emotionless when she said, "I understand." Then she hung up.

"Problems?" Wyatt asked.

She didn't look at him. "Nothing I can't handle," she murmured as she turned another page in the notebook and found another number she needed. She wasn't about to tell him she'd just lost her job at the bar. She didn't blame the manager. She'd put him in a bad spot, giving such short notice, and he'd fired her. She would have to find another evening job when she came back.

As she dialed the third number, she looked up at Wyatt. "Your breakfast is getting cold."

He took the hint reluctantly. She wanted privacy to make her calls, but there was something in her eyes that made him wish she would let him share the burden of making arrangements so she could leave. She was too cool, too matter-of-fact about a situation that had to be causing her some inner turmoil. It wasn't that he wanted a hysterical female on his hands, but her composure was unsettling and unnatural. She was going to see the woman who'd given her up when she was a baby. He didn't think it would be unnatural if she was a little bitter toward Delta. And curious. Or something.

It wasn't that she was unfeeling and emotionless. He'd felt her response when he'd kissed her, seen the flashes of temper in her green eyes, glimpsed a vulnerability in her expression when she'd been sleeping and her guard was down.

Maybe he'd been expecting her to be more like Delta, who was the most open, outspoken person he'd ever known. Aside from her eccentric habit of sleeping during the day and working at night, the artist was very predictable. If she didn't like something, she said so. She shared her opinions whether they were wanted or not.

Cassandra Mason was a closed book.

He was drying a plate after washing his dishes when she entered the kitchen. She held out her hand toward him. "Could I have my keys, please?"

He caught a glimpse of a small purse hanging from her shoulder. "Where are you going?"

Striving for patience, Cass spoke slowly and carefully. "I told you I had things to take care of before I left."

He dug into the pocket of his jeans and withdrew her key ring. "I'll go with you," he said, handing it to her.

For a moment she simply looked at him, surprise widening her eyes. Then she repeated what she'd said earlier. "I'll handle it." She glanced at her watch. "I don't know how long I'll be. Perhaps it would be better if I just met you at the airport before the flight."

She took it for granted he would agree and turned to leave the kitchen. She went into her bedroom to check for anything she might have forgotten. When she walked out a minute later, Wyatt was standing in the kitchen doorway. As she passed him, he grabbed her shoulder and turned her around.

Wyatt ignored the flash of temper in her eyes. Placing both hands on her shoulders, he was suddenly aware of the fragile feel of her. "Let me help, Cass. I'm responsible for putting you in this position. Just tell me what needs to be done, and I'll help you do it."

She shook her head vehemently. "I can ha—"

His fingers tightened, and he gave her a slight shake. "If you say you can handle it one more time, I'm going to throttle you. There's no need for you to handle everything alone."

She wished he would release her. The temptation to lean on him was strong, and that was something she couldn't do. She was on her own, as she'd been all her life. It wasn't necessarily the way she'd wanted it, but it was the way it was and had always been. She was a realist if nothing else.

Stiffening her spine and her resolve, she met his intense gaze. "I appreciate your offer, but the things I have to do can only be done by me. If you want to stay here until the flight, I don't mind. Just turn the lock before you leave."

He ignored her attempt to pull away from him. Instead he took her upper arm and led her toward the door, picking up her suitcase with his free hand. "I'm going with you."

She balked. "I don't want you to come with me."

He smiled down at her. "You've made that perfectly clear."

She opened her mouth to protest, but before she could speak, he lowered his head and gave her a brief, hard kiss. Then he lifted his head, took her hand, and drew her out of her apartment.

"Come on," he said when she continued to hold back. "We're wasting time. We'll take my rental car and leave yours here."

Giving up, Cass walked beside him toward his car parked by the curb. "What is Key West doing for a steamroller now that you're here?" she asked sweetly.

He grinned down at her as he opened the passenger door for her. "I've learned in our short acquaintance that being subtle doesn't work with you. Ignoring your protests does." His eyes glittered with amusement. "I've also learned that kissing you is a very pleasant way to shut you up."

When he walked around to the driver's side, she almost stomped her foot in frustration. Aside from being a childish thing to do, she doubted it would make any difference. If she hadn't had the appointment with Myra's doctor, she would have taken the time to set Wyatt Brodie straight about his dictatorial attitude.

And demand that he stop kissing her.

Cass thought Wyatt would be bored and restless waiting for her while she talked to Myra's doctor, but when she came out of the doctor's office, Wyatt was entertaining a little girl by reading a book to her. When he looked up and saw Cass, he handed the child back to her mother and joined Cass.

Instead of taking her arm as usual, he threaded his fingers through hers. There was no amusement in his voice or his eyes as he looked down at her and asked, "How'd it go?"

Her first impulse was to give him an evasive answer, as she did with anyone who asked about her private life. It was a contest as to who was more surprised, him or her, when she answered, "Dr. Travis doesn't think my going away will affect Myra adversely at this point."

"Are we going to see Myra next?" Wyatt asked as he pushed open the heavy glass door of the clinic.

The fact that he automatically included himself didn't bother her as much as it should. "No," she said flatly. Then realizing she was being rude, she explained, "During this stage of her treatment she isn't supposed to have visitors. The doctor said she needs to learn to depend on herself."

Walking beside her, Wyatt thought it was an odd way for a patient to be treated, but he didn't question Cass about it. Instead he asked, "Where do you need to go next?"

She slipped on a pair of sunglasses, as much to protect her eyes from the bright sunlight as to shield her expression from him. It wouldn't do to let him see how vulnerable she was to his attention.

"To the bank, then the airport."

Apparently she wasn't going to wait to cash his check, he mused. He glanced down at her. She was obviously deep in thought, and he knew it wouldn't do him any good to ask what she was thinking about.

Cass was reminding herself not to count on Wyatt's support. She would be in Key West for just two weeks. After that she'd have no reason to see Wyatt Brodie again. To become involved with him even in her own mind would be foolish and could only lead to heartbreak. It would be easy for her to believe his attentiveness was caused by his guilt for more or less forcing her to go to Key West. Yet he truly seemed to want to make the transition easier for her, even if the only thing he could do was drive her where she wanted to go and wait for her to finish.

He had no way of knowing that no one had ever done either for her before.

Cass heard their flight being called and began to gather her purse and the stack of magazines Wyatt had bought at one of the kiosks at the Gulfport airport. He had turned his rental car in before buying their tickets, refusing to let her buy her own. It was the first time she'd seen him lose his temper. As soon as she'd given in and allowed him to buy her ticket, he'd given her a smile that had curled her insides.

When she stood up, she found him next to her. Instead of striding toward the gate, though, he took her hand and held her in place.

His eyes were serious as he looked down at her. "I know it won't be easy meeting your mother after such a long time. I want you to know that you can come to me if there are any problems, and I'll try to do what I can to help you."

She started to give him her pat answer, "I can handle it," but stopped when she saw the flash of irritation in his eyes. Changing her statement, she said, "I'll remember that."

Thinking that was all he wanted to say, she started to turn, but he didn't move. Staring up at him, she waited.

"One more thing." His voice was low and serious. "Having you see your mother again isn't the only reason I want you to come to Key West."

He kissed her briefly but thoroughly. "Think about it."

Four

Even though he hadn't requested that someone pick them up at the airport, Wyatt wasn't surprised to see Connie's nephew waiting for them at the baggage claim. It took Wyatt a few seconds to remember the man's name, since the list of friends and relatives of the Haitian housekeeper was long and varied. Clovis, he recalled as he clasped the other man's hand.

Wyatt noticed that Clovis gave Cass a few curious glances after he introduced them and set about gathering their luggage. He had no idea what Connie might have told Clovis about the woman accompanying Wyatt back to the island. The phone call he'd made from the Gulfport airport had been brief. He'd only told Connie he was bringing Cass back with him. That was all he'd had to say.

It was rare for Wyatt to leave the island, much less to bring a woman back with him. He could understand Clovis's speculative glances at her.

He'd given little thought to how curious people would be about Cass and what connotation they might put on her visit to Delta's house.

It didn't bother him if Clovis or anyone else thought he'd brought Cass back for his own personal reasons. It was partly true. He'd meant what he'd said to her before they left Biloxi. Delta might have been the reason he'd come looking for her, but reuniting Cass with her mother was no longer his only motivation in bringing her to Key West. She stirred feelings deep inside him that were unfamiliar. He needed to figure out exactly what they were.

Cass caught the frown on Wyatt's face and wondered what caused it. She'd seen the other man glance at Wyatt's arm around her waist, seen the curious gleam in his dark eyes. She'd also been aware of the moment Wyatt removed his arm after she shook hands with Clovis. A thread of anger wove its way into her mind. If Wyatt didn't want people to get the wrong idea of their relationship, he shouldn't touch her with the familiarity that seemed normal to him, but was unusual for her.

Apparently that thought had occurred to him as well, since he was no longer touching her. They were back on his home turf, where people knew him. It wasn't the same as being anonymous in Biloxi. She couldn't stop the feeling of betrayal his change in attitude caused. What had she expected? she asked herself. He'd accomplished his mission. She was in Key West. He no longer needed to use his powers of persuasion to get her there. It wasn't a problem, she concluded. She could handle it.

She was silent during the ride to Delta's large

wood-frame house. During the short trip she noticed that Wyatt stared out the side window, although the view had to be familiar to him. She didn't realize how much she had relied on his support until it had been withdrawn.

The house looked exactly as she remembered it. She counted the green rocking chairs on the porch, finding there were eight, the same number as before. Shrubs, flowers, and palm trees hugged the house, and a white picket fence surrounded the property, except for the space allowing cars to use the paved driveway. A feeling of déjà vu swept over her as she thought about the time she'd first seen the house ten years ago. It had been like a scene in one of the books she'd read about a tropical paradise.

Until she'd overheard Delta talking to Connie.

Clovis turned into the driveway and parked near the back door. At the end of the long driveway was Delta's studio with its panels of glass built into the roof to allow light inside. Cass remembered thinking how strange it was that Delta's studio would have skylights when the artist always painted at night. She also remembered how much light they'd provided when she herself had used the studio during her visit ten years ago.

Wyatt was about to get out of the taxi when he caught the expression on Cass's face as she stared at the studio. Sadness, regret, yearning, and bitterness flickered in her expressive eyes before she looked away. He would have given a great deal to know her thoughts. Whatever they were, they weren't happy.

Connie Dubacca opened the back door as they

approached it and held out a hand to Cass. "Come in, child," she invited in her soft, accented voice. Her glance slid to Wyatt. "Mr. Wyatt, you help Clovis with the luggage, then join us for tea."

"Yes, ma'am," he said, grinning at the older woman's direction.

Cass followed Connie into the kitchen. As she quickly glanced around, she could have sworn nothing had changed here either. She might have been gone only ten days instead of ten years. Even the scent of spices and baking was familiar after all this time.

The numerous bracelets Connie always wore jangled pleasantly as the housekeeper picked up a fully laden tray off a table near one of the windows. "We'll have tea on the porch," she said as she started out of the kitchen, toward the front of the house, "to give you a moment to catch your breath before I take you up to your room. Then you will see Miss Delta."

As Cass trailed after Connie, she realized Connie hadn't referred to Delta as Aunt Delta, which was what Cass had called her before. Nor had Connie said "your mother."

Once they reached the porch, Connie set the tray down on one of the small tables and indicated with a sweep of her hand for Cass to be seated in the green rocking chair on the other side of the table.

Cass expected to have a flurry of questions fired at her, but Connie simply poured their tea and sat back in her chair, rocking gently back and forth. Gradually Cass relaxed as she sipped the tea, grateful for the moment of peace. It was as if

Connie knew how badly she needed time to accustom herself to her surroundings.

When Wyatt joined them a few minutes later, he half-sat on the porch railing, facing her. She could see he was relaxed and at ease. This was his home in a way that it never would be hers. He belonged here, and she never had.

With one of her graceful gestures Connie indicated the tea tray. "Would you care for a cup of tea, Mr. Wyatt?"

He shook his head. "No, thanks. Did you tell Delta we were arriving today?"

Connie nodded her head once. "She knows."

"How's Salem? The last time I talked to her, she said she was fine, but there was something in her voice that said otherwise."

"She is nearing her time. There are discomforts."

Cass set her cup down. It was obvious Wyatt was eager to catch up on all the news concerning the people he cared about, and she felt like an intruder. Placing her hands on the arms of the chair, she stood up. "If you'll excuse me, I believe I'll go to my room, if you'll tell me which one I've been assigned."

Wyatt examined her face closely. Her eyes gave nothing away. "Stay. You haven't finished your tea."

She shook her head. "You and Connie have a lot to talk about." Looking at Connie, she asked, "Which room would you like me to use?" When she saw the housekeeper start to stand, she said, "Please. There's no need for you to go with me. Will I be using the same room I had before?"

Connie's eyes were dark and penetrating. "Miss

Delta would like you to use Miss Salem's old room. It's the one next to hers."

Cass steeled herself not to give her feelings away. With an abrupt nod of her head, she walked over to the door and entered the house.

Wyatt kept his gaze on the closed screen door for a long moment. Then he stepped away from the railing and sank down into the chair Cass had occupied. "She feels like an outsider."

"It is understandable. It's how she's been treated."

Wyatt heard the note of censure in Connie's voice and wondered whether it was directed toward Delta or the situation in general. "You knew about her, didn't you? All along you've known of her relationship to Delta."

"I've known." She pinned her dark gaze on Wyatt's face. "It is not for me to make judgments on others' lives."

He took the statement in the spirit it was given, not offended. "I'm not making judgments about Delta or anyone else. I just don't like the way this has been handled, and I'm partly responsible for that. Cass is the innocent victim, the one paying for the past."

"There are many adjustments for her to make inside herself. Learning Miss Delta was her mother must have been a shock to her."

"Not as much as you think," he murmured. "She already knew."

Connie stared at him, astonishment widening her eyes. "I didn't think Miss Mason would have told her."

"She didn't. Cass somehow learned about it when she was here ten years ago."

Sitting back in her chair, Connie sighed heavily. "That explains the change in her that summer. The day she arrived, she was smiling, excited about her visit. Later she became quiet and withdrawn. Miss Delta thought she was simply homesick. I wonder why she never confronted Miss Delta then."

"That's not her style," Wyatt said. Using the phrase that seemed to be Cass's motto, he added in a dry tone, "She handled it."

He proceeded to tell Connie what he knew about Cass's life in Biloxi, what little she had told him and the things he'd found out from her co-workers, which wasn't all that much.

When he finished, Connie asked, "Did you see Miss Mason while you were there?"

He shook his head. "She's not staying with Cass. Right before we left, Cass talked to Miss Mason's doctor at the clinic where she's a patient. Cass didn't say why Myra was still being hospitalized, but while she was in with the doctor, I learned from a woman in the waiting room that the clinic specializes in treating people for substance abuse."

"Miss Cassandra has not had an easy time of it, it seems," Connie said quietly.

Wyatt felt that was a gross understatement, but didn't say so. Levering his long body out of the chair, he asked, "When is she going to see Delta?"

Connie also stood up. "If Miss Delta is awake now, I will take Miss Cassandra in to see her."

"I'd like to do it." A corner of his mouth curved upward in a rueful smile when Connie looked at him with raised brows. "I got her into this by bringing her here. The least I can do is be with her the first time they meet as mother and daughter. I'll go speak with Delta first, then take Cass in to her, if that's all right with you."

Connie gazed at him for several moments without saying a word. Then she simply nodded. Taking the tray with her, she walked to the door Wyatt held open for her.

Cass sat on the padded window seat in Salem Shepherd's old bedroom. Her suitcase had been placed on a stand at the foot of the brass bed, but she hadn't opened it. She didn't want to unpack her things. When she'd first stepped into the room, she'd been tempted to go back downstairs and ask Connie if she could possibly have another room. She felt like an interloper there.

It didn't seem right for her to be in that room. Not in Salem's old room. Salem had been the beloved daughter of the house, not her. Maybe Delta was ready to accept her as her daughter, but it wasn't that easy for Cass to shift into the role after all this time.

She turned her head toward the door when it opened. Expecting to see Connie, she tensed when she saw Wyatt standing in the doorway instead.

"Are you all right?" he asked.

"Of course."

His smile was mocking. "Of course," he echoed. "Nothing throws Cassandra Mason, does it? At least not very far or for very long."

She continued to look at him, keeping her expression blank with an effort. He had no idea how thrown she really was by being there, and she certainly wasn't going to tell him. Thankful her pride kept her from allowing any of her apprehension to show, she asked, "Did you want something?"

There was a flicker in the depths of his eyes, then it was gone. "A loaded question if I ever heard one," he murmured. "Delta is awake and would like to see you."

She nodded and rose from the window seat. "All right."

He didn't move out of her way as she approached him. Lifting his hand, he allowed himself the pleasure of running the back of his fingers down the side of her neck. "I haven't thanked you for coming back with me. I know the decision wasn't easy for you."

Afraid her eyes would reveal her heated response to his touch, she concentrated on one of the buttons on his shirt. "There's no need. It's something I should have done a long time ago."

Placing his finger under her chin, he forced her to look up at him. Her lashes raised slowly, revealing her sultry green eyes as she met his gaze. "I know you're used to fighting your own battles, Cass. I want you to know this is one you don't have to fight on your own. I'm responsible for bringing you here, and I'm not abandoning you now that you are here."

She didn't want to be his responsibility. She didn't know what she did want from him, but it wasn't that. "I made the choice to come. You don't have to feel as though you forced me."

His hands settled at her waist. "That's important to you, isn't it? Having a choice."

She tried to control a shiver of awareness at his

touch, but she was afraid she wasn't very successful. "Isn't it important to you to have the choice of how you live your life? Wasn't that one of the reasons you ran away from the orphanage, because you had no choice there about how you lived? I would say that making your own decisions is just as important to you. Why do you expect it to be any different with me?"

"Sometimes our choices are taken away from us by something stronger than our own wills," he said quietly. He drew her closer. "Take what's happening between us."

She didn't deny there was something growing between them. "I've already decided what to do about that," she said.

He could have bet this month's profits it wasn't the same thing he planned to do. "What have you decided?"

"It's like craving chocolate. If I ignore it long enough, it will go away."

He chuckled softly as he slid his hands over her hips, bringing them against his. He watched her eyes change as she became aware of his hardening body. "I'm not sure this will go away simply by ignoring it. It's like trying to ignore a hurricane when it's whirling all around you."

The evidence of his reaction to her was obvious and potent, and Cass gasped as his hard arousal pressed against her. She instinctively shifted her hips, seeking relief but finding that the action only made the need stronger. When she realized what she was doing, she froze.

Wyatt felt her stiffen and loosened his hold on her, just enough for their bodies to separate. It wasn't what he wanted, but it was the only thing he could do at the moment. He wanted to kiss her, feel her mouth under his. It wouldn't be enough, but it would be an outlet for the need coiling through him.

When he saw the glazed expression in her eyes as she lifted her head, his hands tightened on her waist. He struggled to quell the desire raging through him.

"You were saying?" he asked, his voice raw and husky.

She leaned her forehead against his chest for a moment, strangely weary, as though she'd been fighting a tough battle up a steep hill. And had lost. The need to be in his arms was too compelling.

Wyatt sensed her withdrawal. As much as he wanted to pursue whatever was growing between them, he remembered why he had come to her room. Again lifting her chin with his hand, he gazed searchingly into her eyes. "Delta's waiting to see you."

She nodded. "I'm ready."

He studied her expression, fascinated by the way she seemed to gather her strength. And she was strong. Apparently she'd had to be for a long time. She didn't expect anyone's help, and he wasn't sure she would accept his, so he didn't offer it. He would just provide it.

She stopped in the doorway and glanced back over her shoulder into the room. "Do you think Connie would mind if I asked for a different room?"

He gave her a puzzled look. "Why? Don't you like this one?"

"It isn't that," she said hesitantly, unwilling to

tell him why she was uncomfortable using Salem's room.

"What is it, then?"

She knew him well enough by now to realize he would keep hammering away until he got his answer. "This is Salem's room," she said by way of explanation.

Remembering his own words to Connie about Cass feeling like an outsider, he said quietly, "She's not going to be using it. She hasn't since she and John got married. Now it's simply a guest room. You're a guest. Why shouldn't you use it?"

Cass squared her shoulders as his words sank in. Now she knew her status in the household. She was a guest, not a member of the family.

Wyatt could feel her tension, yet was helpless to ease it. "Cass?"

She stepped into the hall and turned in the direction of Delta's room without answering him. His hand went to the small of her back and remained there as he walked beside her down the hall. When they reached Delta's bedroom, he rapped softly twice before opening the door. He ushered Cass into the room ahead of him, giving her the silent support of his hand at her waist as he guided her to a chair beside the bed.

The drapes were partially open, letting in enough sun to lighten the room. As Cass walked across the plush beige carpet, her gaze fixed on the woman propped up against a number of pillows on the bed. It was the first time Cass had ever been in Delta's bedroom, but she wasn't interested in the furnishings. All of her attention was centered on the woman lying in the bed.

Delta's faded blond hair was brushed away from

her face and plaited into a single braid. The dynamic woman Cass remembered seemed diminished somehow, smaller and more fragile. She was wearing a soft blue bedjacket, her hands folded on top of the sheet. Slender plastic tubing was attached to an oxygen cylinder beside the bed and was held under Delta's nose by a length of elastic around her neck.

Delta's eyes never left Cass's face, their expression a combination of curiosity, apprehension, and pleasure. "Thank you for coming, Cassandra. I wasn't sure you would."

Cass managed a smile. "You sent a persuasive messenger."

Delta shifted her glance to Wyatt, who was still standing beside Cass. "Thank you, Wyatt. I knew I could count on you." Bringing her gaze back to Cass, she asked, "Would you sit down, Cassandra? The sun is behind you, and I can't see you clearly."

When Cass sat in the chair, Wyatt walked over to the door. Instead of leaving, he leaned back against it, his gaze remaining on Cass. She wasn't sure whether he was staying for Delta's sake or hers. It could be a combination of both. He could be making sure she didn't do or say anything that would upset Delta. Under the circumstances Cass couldn't blame him. His first loyalty would be to the woman who had taken him in years ago, not a woman he'd just met.

"How are you, Delta?" she asked.

The older woman smiled wanly. "Never better," she said, then ruined the optimistic statement by coughing.

Cass frowned as she listened to Delta's labored

breathing. "Perhaps I should leave. I can come back when you're feeling better."

"No," Delta said hoarsely. "Just give me a minute."

Cass turned to look beseechingly at Wyatt. He knew Delta's health situation. If he thought she should leave, she would.

He hadn't moved. His stance was relaxed, his expression as calm as usual. Then he smiled and winked at her. She should stay.

Typical of Delta's straightforward approach to life, she didn't waste time in meaningless polite conversation. Once she caught her breath, she said, "I've spent many hours trying to figure out the best way to tell you the facts of your birth. I recently learned it isn't necessary. I understand from Wyatt you've known for a long time."

Cass simply nodded.

"Somehow you found out when you were here when you were seventeen, didn't you?"

This time Cass answered. "Yes."

"I've often wondered," Delta said after a moment's pause. "Your attitude changed so drastically that summer."

Seeing the older woman's pallor, Cass said gently, "Delta, we don't need to talk about this now. Wyatt told me you've been very ill. Perhaps we should wait until you're a little stronger. Or we don't have to talk about it at all."

Delta shook her head, her lips forming a slight smile. "I doubt if I will ever be as strong as I would like to be to discuss this, but I need to find some peace with myself. And maybe even with you. Please tell me how you discovered I'm your mother and not Myra."

Cass once again looked over her shoulder at Wyatt to see if she should answer. He smiled again, and this time nodded in encouragement. She returned her attention to Delta. "The third day I was here I overheard you talking to Connie. You told her that since you'd seen me, you were positive you'd done the right thing by handing me over to your best friend to raise so that you could go to France to study art."

Delta flinched, and her lips parted as she inhaled a deep breath of air. "There were kinder ways for you to hear the truth. I'm sorry you had to find out that way. It explains why you closed yourself off for the remainder of your visit and refused ever to return." She paused to catch her breath. "Why didn't you confront me with what you heard then?"

Cass looked steadily at the older woman, wondering how much honesty Delta really wanted. "It was a long time ago. I've accepted things the way they are. Let's leave it at that."

"All right," the artist replied heavily. "For now. How is Myra? I would like to see her again, to thank her for all she's done for you. She used to be so good about writing to me, telling me how you were, what you were doing, sending me pictures. I haven't heard from her in a long time, and I've been worried about her. And you."

"She has a few health problems," Cass answered evasively.

"I suppose at our age it's to be expected. I hope it's nothing serious."

"She was in a car accident a couple of years ago. There were complications."

Delta wasn't satisfied with Cass's vague answer.

"What kind of complications?" When Cass didn't answer, she said with a hint of her normal spirit, "I might be under the weather at the moment, but I haven't suddenly lost my senses. I would rather know what has happened to Myra than be left in the dark."

Cass debated how much to tell Delta about Myra's condition. She bit her lip, then decided there had been enough lies and half-truths between her and the woman lying on the bed. There was also a chance refusing to tell Delta the truth might upset her even more than the truth would.

"Myra is in a clinic recovering from alcohol and drug abuse, Delta," she said quietly. "While hospitalized with injuries from a car accident, she became dependent on medication." Cass hesitated, then added, "She was already addicted to alcohol."

Delta didn't speak for a few minutes. "I was afraid it was something like that," she said finally, sighing. "I knew she had a tendency to drink too much, but I didn't realize it was that serious. Her letters had become progressively disjointed over the years, then she stopped writing altogether. I had my suspicions when I tried to call and discovered her phone was disconnected. The letters I sent came back to me. How long has she had a drinking problem?"

"A few years," Cass said obliquely.

"Will she be all right?"

"I don't know. It will be up to her. She's receiving counseling at the clinic. It depends on whether she wants to recover or not."

"You should have contacted me. There might have been something I could do to help. Why didn't you let me know?" She held up her hand to halt Cass's answer. "Never mind. I don't have the right to ask that," she said wearily. Delta watched Cass for a long moment, then asked, "Would you like me to tell you about your father?"

"It's not necessary."

Delta's eyes darkened. With surprise? Disappointment? Cass didn't know her well enough to be able to read her expression.

"How long will you stay?" Delta asked.

Cass noticed she had phrased the question to make it clear she knew it was Cass's decision how long she would stay. "Two weeks. I can't be away from my job any longer than that." Seeing the strain in Delta's eyes, she stood up, but remained beside the bed. "We can talk again later after you've had some rest."

Delta raised her hand toward her. "I'm glad you're here, Cassandra. I'm not going to ask your forgiveness, because I still believe I did the right thing. What you heard me say ten years ago was based on the fact that you seemed well adjusted and happy living with Myra. That's why I thought I'd done what was best by leaving you with her. I'm going to ask that we try to become friends. I hope you will agree eventually."

Cass took the older woman's hand in her own, aware of the frail fingers she held gently in her grasp. "I haven't come as an enemy, Delta. I would like to get to know you better. Perhaps in the next couple of weeks we can accomplish that."

Delta nodded and released Cass's hand, then looked at Wyatt. "Salem and John will be here for dinner, if Salem is feeling up to it. I would like you also to be present."

He nodded in agreement, then opened the door, waiting for Cass to leave the room. She expected him to stay and talk with Delta, but instead he stepped into the hall after her, closed the door, and caught up with her in two long strides. He grabbed her hand and continued toward Salem's bedroom, pulling her after him.

Surprised at his strong-arm tactics, she resisted. "What are you doing?"

He didn't answer her. He shoved open the door of her room and drew her inside. After shutting the door, he took hold of her shoulders to keep her in front of him.

"Why didn't you tell me?" he asked.

Her eyes showed her confusion as she looked up at him. "Tell you what?"

"About Myra. You gave me the impression she was recovering from injuries from an accident."

"She is."

"And alcoholism," he reminded her. "Becoming an alcoholic isn't an overnight thing. You had plenty of opportunity to tell me the last three days, especially when we went to the clinic, but you didn't. I'd like to know why." Seeing her confusion change to bewilderment, he eased his grip on her shoulders, his thumbs smoothing over the delicate bones. "You're so used to facing everything on your own, it never occurred to you to tell anyone, did it? You handled it. Right? All by yourself, without asking anyone for help. Whenever I asked about her, you never once implied her problems were more serious than recovering from the accident. You're even paying for her care, aren't you? That's why you're working two jobs."

His anger was fueling her own. "What else was I supposed to do? She needed help. I'm all she has."

"You didn't have to deal with it alone."

She broke away from him and stepped back, planting her hands on her hips. "The first time she passed out on the living room floor, I was ten years old. I looked around. There was no one else there. There never was. I did what had to be done."

"And you still are," he said as he moved toward her. She was trying to keep him at a distance, but it wasn't going to work. He pulled her into his arms and simply held her. "You aren't alone any longer. You might as well get used to that."

She didn't know what he meant, but she didn't push him away again. It felt too good to be in his arms. So much had happened so fast, so many changes in her life during the last couple of days, it was a relief to lean on someone. If only for a brief time. She wasn't going to make a habit of it. No matter what Wyatt was promising, she didn't expect him or anyone else to take on her problems.

It might be natural for him to share his life with others, but she'd never had that luxury. It was foreign territory. There had never been anyone she could trust, anyone she felt would always be there. She didn't expect coming back as Delta's daughter would change that.

She was aware of the moment his intent changed. His hands began to smooth over her, slowly and gently at first, until the curves of her body enticed him to explore and caress.

She trembled and made a soft sound deep in her throat. "Wyatt?"

He raised his head and gazed down into her eyes, seeing arousal flare in their depths. Eyes a man could drown in, he mused.

"Don't shut me out, Cass," he murmured, then lowered his head to take her mouth.

Five

Cass wasn't sure whether he meant he didn't want her shutting him out of her life or from the intimacy of her mouth. She didn't get a chance to wonder about it. When she felt the abrasive stroke of his tongue against hers, she couldn't think at all.

Her fingers clutched his shirt as desire spiraled through her. Under her hand she felt his strong heartbeat, and she felt her own accelerate as she was overwhelmed with his taste, his warmth, his masculine scent. She shuddered when he thrust his hips against her, his hand at the small of her back forcing her to feel how she affected him. He was hard and potent, vitally male. Unable to think, she could only react, reveling in his mouth working magic on hers, his aroused manhood pressing against her.

It wasn't like her to give in to the selfish needs of her body so easily, so naturally. Fear blended with the aching hunger he was creating within her. The way he made her feel scared her as nothing else ever had. He aroused a throbbing emptiness deep inside her that was filled with a nameless longing. The contradiction was difficult to fight, to feel. His kiss was hard, then soft, then deep, searching, satisfying her yearning.

When he broke away from her mouth, he buried his face in her neck, his breathing ragged against her skin. She felt his body shudder as he held her close.

He was holding her so tightly, she had difficulty breathing. Or perhaps it was because of the riotous sensations raging through her that made it so difficult to pull vital air into her lungs. He literally took her breath away, and all he'd had to do was touch her.

Slowly, regretfully, Wyatt raised his head, loosening his hold on her. His strong hands held her waist to steady her and himself as he gazed down into her glazed eyes. He hadn't meant to kiss her. All he'd planned to do was talk to her, and get her to talk to him. His frustrations had been eclipsed by the need to touch her, though. Unable to make her respond to him in any other way, he'd tried to get closer to her physically. He wasn't going to apologize for kissing her, because he wasn't sorry.

Satisfaction filled him, for even if she could hide her thoughts from him, she couldn't hide her response when he kissed her. It was a start. Heat throbbed through him as he remembered the feel of her in his arms, her body grinding against him. One helluva start.

Cass felt heat rise in waves at the intense sensual warmth in Wyatt's eyes. Unclenching her fingers, she laid her palms flat across his chest, feeling the thud of his heartbeat. She also felt a hard circular piece of metal and traced it with her fingers. "What's this?"

His hand dipped into the shirt, one finger hooked a chain, and he drew out a medallion the size of a nickel. "It's a two-escudo piece from the first treasure hunt John ever went on. He had necklaces made for the three of us."

Cass ran a finger over the antique coin, then she slowly stepped back. His hands dropped away, and she wrapped her arms around her waist as she walked over to the window. Staring out at the profusion of plants that bordered Delta's property, she said quietly, "I haven't had much experience talking about my private life. Shutting you or anyone else out isn't intentional." With a ghost of a laugh she added, "Maybe it is. I don't know. I guess I don't expect other people to understand how protecting Myra has become a habit. My life has been so involved with hers, talking about myself would mean talking about her. It's easier not to say anything at all."

When he spoke, she felt his breath on the back of her neck. She had been so involved in her own thoughts, she hadn't realized he had come up behind her.

"I understand more than you think," he murmured. "After three foster homes I was sent to the Children's Home in Boston with a reputation for being a troublemaker. I was so angry at the world, felt so betrayed by people who were supposed to care about me, I refused to speak to anyone for several months. A boy a few years older than me and fifty pounds heavier tried to make me talk by beating the stuffing out of me. He had a bet going with some of the other kids that he could get me to speak, even if it was only to cry out in pain."

Cass jerked around to face him, her eyes wide with shock.

Wyatt let his words touch her instead of his hands. "John pulled him off me and took me behind the boys' dormitory building. I remember leaning against the brick wall. For a long time afterward I could still feel how rough brick scraped my back as I slid down to the ground when my legs gave out. John didn't say a word, just sat down beside me and handed me a handkerchief so that I could wipe the blood off my face. I don't know how long we stayed there. I only remember he never left my side. He didn't give me any long lectures, no long-winded bits of advice, not a single word of either sympathy or ridicule. He was simply there. It was the first time anyone had ever stood up for me without demanding anything in exchange. John was the first person I ever trusted. Salem was the second."

He saw the tears glistening in Cass's eyes, but didn't resent them. They were for the boy, not the man. "It isn't easy to trust someone when you've never had anyone who will stand by you no matter what. You don't know me well enough to trust me yet. That will come. All I'm asking is for you to remember that I'm here if you need me. I won't try to force you into something you aren't ready for."

Emotion made her voice husky as she admitted, "Every time you touch me, you force me to want you."

Stunned, Wyatt stared down at her. Her admission inflamed him, jolting him in a way he'd never felt before. His hand was trembling when he lifted it to touch her hair.

"Boy," he said, his smile a little ragged, "when you finally let go, you land quite a punch."

Having gone that far, Cass didn't back down. Taking her cue from him, she attempted to lighten the atmosphere around them. "Remember that saying about being careful what you ask for?"

He nodded. "Or I might get it. It makes me wonder what will happen when I ask you to go to bed with me."

She tilted her head to one side. "Do you usually move this fast? You've only known me three days."

"I feel like I've known you all my life," he said seriously, realizing he spoke the truth. "I've never wanted anyone as badly as I want you. It's how I've felt since I saw you that first night at Chasen's."

He wrapped a lock of her hair around his finger, the silken strands binding her to him. It wasn't unlike the way he was beginning to feel about her, as though they were bound together by invisible threads.

A muffled sound brought them back to the outside world. A woman's laugh filtered through the walls, making Wyatt smile. "Salem's here."

He automatically reached for Cass's hand to draw her out of the room, but she held back. "You go ahead."

Instead of leaving, he turned to face her. "Come with me."

She shook her head. "I'll be down later. I know you're concerned about Salem right now. Go talk to her."

"If Salem's here, so is John. He won't let her out of his sight. They know you're here. They'll expect to see you too."

"There are bound to be things you want to catch up on with them. I'll only be in the way."

Lacing his fingers through hers, he met her gaze, not at all surprised to see the defensive expression in her eyes. He grinned down at her. "It's not a good idea to upset a pregnant lady. Especially Salem. You haven't lived until you've seen her mad. I'm not brave enough to face her without you."

Cass shook her head and laughed. "I don't believe you're afraid of anything or anyone, but I wouldn't want you to get in trouble in case I'm wrong."

"You've saved my life," he muttered as he led her out of the bedroom.

John and Salem were waiting for them at the bottom of the stairs. Cass recognized John immediately. He was as tan, as rugged, as tall as she remembered him, although there was one change she noticed immediately. He was smiling. During the week she had been on the island, she had never seen him smile. He had always been quiet, tired from overworking, leaving Wyatt and Salem to contribute to the conversation at the dinner table.

Cass's gaze went to his wife, and she found herself smiling. Ten years ago Salem had been a young, spirited girl whose laughter filled the house. Now she was a woman. Gone was the girl with tangled long black hair who never walked when she could run. Her hair was smooth and pulled back into a knot at the base of her neck. Her red gauze maternity dress partly camouflaged her pregnancy, but nothing could disguise the pleasure in her blue eyes as she watched Cass and Wyatt descend the stairs.

The moment her foot reached the floor, Cass was thankful for Wyatt's steadying grip on her hand. Salem immediately hugged her, nearly unbalancing Cass with her excitement and enthusiasm.

After releasing Cass, Salem lunged at Wyatt and gave him a welcoming embrace, along with a kiss on the cheek. "It's about time you got back."

Wyatt grinned. "It's good to see you, too, brat." He shifted his gaze to John. "How are you doing, Papa?"

John smiled. "I'm surviving. So far." To Cass's astonishment, he reached over and briefly hugged her. "Welcome to Key West, Cass. I hope you'll be able to exert some influence over this impossible woman."

Wyatt chuckled. "What's she done now?"

"She wanted to go diving yesterday. The baby is due any minute and she wants to strap on a tank and jump off a boat. If this kid doesn't arrive pretty soon, you might have to run the fleet alone. I'll be in a nice padded cell somewhere blowing bubbles."

Salem lifted her chin. "Ignore him, Cass. I do. I'm so glad you're here. You won't believe what I have to put up with around here. You look won-

derful. Wyatt told me how beautiful you'd become."
She made a face as she scanned Cass's slim figure. "Although I can't help wishing you'd gained
about fifty pounds so I wouldn't be the only one
around here who waddles."

"But you're so cute when you waddle, Salem,"
Wyatt drawled. "Like a plump little green-eyed
duck."

John grinned down at his wife. "More like a
mouthy green-eyed goose."

Salem sighed. "See what I mean? The only consolation I have is they'll both probably get sympathy pains when I start labor."

The two men exchanged rueful looks, then
gazed warily at Salem, their expressions showing
their apprehension, both obviously afraid it might
be true. Laughing, Salem took Cass's arm and led
her toward the dining room, chatting a mile a
minute. Physically she might have had to slow
down, but her conversation was as fast and furious as ever, her laughter contagious.

The laughter was what Cass remembered later.
That and the feeling of companionship as they
all sat around the dining room table eating the
delicious food Connie had prepared. The only sol-
emn moment came when they discussed Delta's
health. Their concern was genuine, their worry
evident, their sense of helplessness apparent.

Hours later Cass threw back the sheet and got
out of bed. Physically she was tired, but her mind
wouldn't shut down and allow sleep to take over.
It had been a long day. Chances were good tomorrow would prove to be just as busy and confusing
as this day had been. When she'd made the decision to come back to Key West, she thought she'd

been prepared. She'd been wrong. She'd been ready for the meeting with Delta, but not the emotion she experienced when she sat down and talked to the woman who had given birth to her. Or the uncomplicated welcome she'd received from John and Salem.

Or the way Wyatt treated her as though it was perfectly natural for him to keep her beside him the whole time John and Salem were there. Even when Salem had gone up to see Delta before they left, Wyatt had insisted Cass go out onto the porch with him and John rather than to her room. Soon after they left, he'd walked her to her room, kissing her all too briefly before gently pushing her through the doorway without saying a word.

Nothing had gone the way she'd expected since she got off the airplane. Delta hadn't apologized for giving her away. Connie treated her as though she'd always been there. Salem had never met a stranger and acted accordingly with Cass. John's attention all evening was mostly on his wife, but he'd never once made Cass feel she didn't belong.

That was the main problem, she thought as she walked slowly over to the window. She was beginning to feel like she did belong there.

As she looked out the window, she saw the shadowy shape of the studio through the leaves of a banyan tree. Staring at the building, she decided to investigate Delta's studio. Maybe her paintings would reveal more about the woman than Cass would be able to learn by talking to her. After she'd overheard the conversation between Delta and Connie, she hadn't been able to go to the studio. Now she found she was curious to see Delta's work. Maybe she would find a clue as to why Delta had put her painting before a human life. It was possible all of Delta's finished work was in the gallery Myra had said Delta had opened on the island. It was also possible some paintings in progress were still in the studio.

Cass opened her suitcase and grabbed the first thing on top. She buttoned the waistband of the short denim skirt before slipping on a white T-shirt that was several sizes too big. Since she wasn't expecting to see anyone, she didn't bother brushing her hair.

Leaving her sandals in her room, she walked barefoot down the stairs and through the kitchen. There was enough natural light from the full moon shining through the windows to prevent her from banging a toe or tripping over any furniture. She let herself out the back door, shutting it carefully behind her.

She followed the path to the studio, reaching up to brush away several limbs that badly needed to be pruned. It was the first indication she had that the path hadn't been used for a while. It hadn't occurred to her the studio might be locked until she reached the door. Since she was there, she gave it a try. To her amazement, the knob turned in her hand.

Stepping inside, she felt around for a light switch near the door and flicked it on. As she gazed at the large cluttered room, her first impression was that the studio looked exactly as it had ten years ago. The odor of paint and turpentine hung in the air, adding to the scent of dust and staleness. The main studio easel was in its usual position. A number of stretched canvases were stacked against one wall. The shelves were as overflowing with painting supplies and assorted props as she remembered. The couch and chairs arranged in an informal sitting area were the same, even the length of material thrown over the worn couch was the floral print she had sat on ten years ago.

The one thing that was noticeably different was the coating of dust on everything. Although the studio had always been somewhat disorganized, it had also been clean. Cass had assumed Connie was the one who kept the studio dust free, until late one night she'd seen Delta down on her hands and knees scrubbing the wood floor. Delta had explained how she often thought a painting through while whisking a dust cloth around the studio or mopping the floor.

Cass felt grit under her bare feet as she slowly walked over to the easel. A palette with globs of dried paint rested on the high table next to the easel, several brushes lying across it. A once-white cloth was draped over the large canvas on the easel. Apparently Delta had been working on it before she became ill.

Cass lifted the cloth and threw it back to expose the painting. She stared. The figure of a young girl standing on a sandy beach was sketched in with broad strokes of expertly applied paint. The background of sea and palm trees was only implied. The face of the girl drew Cass's gaze.

The face was the only completed part of the painting. And the face was hers.

"It was done from memory."

Cass whirled around. Wyatt was leaning against the door frame, watching her. His hands were shoved into the front pockets of his jeans, his shirt was open, and he wore deck shoes without socks. He had the look of a man who had dressed quickly, or had been in the process of undressing.

When her heartbeat steadied enough for her to speak without showing how much the sight of him affected her, she said, "I thought you said you lived in a cottage down by the marina."

"I do. I saw the light on in the studio from my window on the third floor. I'm staying here temporarily."

"Because I'm here?"

"That's part of it." He didn't say what the other part was. Pushing his lean body away from the doorway, he walked toward her. When he stopped beside her, he studied the painting. "Delta started this about six months ago after her first serious asthma attack. We all tried to get her to rest, but she kept coming out here to work on it."

"Why then? I could understand it if she had painted it shortly after I left ten years ago, but not six months ago."

"You were apparently on her mind. As outspoken as Delta is, she lets her paintings say a great deal that she can't put into words. She appears to be one tough lady, but she has soft spots she doesn't let others see." He glanced down at her. "You have that in common."

Still looking at the painting, Cass murmured, "Do you think you've known me long enough to form opinions about what I'm like?"

He smiled. "I notice you didn't deny what I said."

Cass didn't want to look at the painting any

longer. "I'm not at my best at one o'clock in the morning."

"I'll have to remember that," he drawled.

She stepped around the easel, walking over to the couch, and sank down onto the well-worn cushions. Drawing her knees up, she wrapped her arms around them and stared at the back of the canvas.

There was plenty of room for two people on the long couch, but Wyatt sat down close beside her. Stretching his long legs out in front of him, he leaned back and released his breath in a long sigh. "Since I've met you, I've forgotten what it's like to sleep."

"Conscience bothering you?"

He chuckled. "My conscience isn't the part that refuses to rest."

Cass couldn't stop the rush of sensual heat. It was scary the way he could make her senses come alive, but she was growing accustomed to the myriad sensations he created within her. In fact she was beginning to wonder how she had ever managed to get through a day without the awareness she experienced when she was with Wyatt.

She turned her head to look at him. His eyes were closed, his breathing slow and even, but she knew he wasn't asleep. "I didn't come to Key West to have an affair with you, Wyatt."

He opened his eyes and met her gaze. "Why did you come? You never did tell me why you changed your mind."

"Where we've come from has a lot to do with where we are today and where we're going tomorrow. I want to know who Delta is. Why she's the way she is. If you were given a chance to learn about the people responsible for giving you life, wouldn't you take advantage of it?"

"Probably."

"That's why I changed my mind. I decided it was time to find out why Delta handed me over to her best friend. That's the reason I came to Key West, not to get involved with you."

"Fair enough. It wasn't what I had in mind either when I went to Biloxi. Now I'm obsessed with thoughts of how it would be to make love with you. It doesn't make for a restful night."

She smiled when she heard his martyred sigh. "Have you tried a cold shower?"

"Believe me, they're grossly overrated."

She was tempted. Lord, was she tempted. He was the first man who'd ever had this effect on her, and she couldn't explain why she felt such a strong attraction. It was like a loud thunderstorm with lightning bolts when he touched her. Rain was inevitable. She could still run for cover before she became drenched. Or drowned.

"Tell me about Delta," she said. "What was she like when the three of you first came to the island?"

"Changing the subject, Cassandra?"

She met his gaze and saw the resigned amusement in his eyes. "Yes."

"I didn't realize you were the cowardly type."

"Now you know. Answer my question, please."

His chest rose and fell as he took in deep breaths. "She was a combination fairy godmother and Mary Poppins. When we arrived on the island, we fell asleep in John's car, which just happened to be parked in front of her house. She found us and invited us in for breakfast instead of sending us on our way. To supplement her income, she took in tourists as paying guests, but there were a couple of rooms on the third floor vacant. Before we had a chance to decide what we were going to do next, she had assigned us rooms. Connie got John a job at one of her relatives' fish markets, and I worked as bait boy on a fishing boat on the weekends. She prodded Salem and me to go to school, and made arrangements for John to take a test so that he could get a high school diploma. A while after John managed to buy his own boat, he and I moved to the cottage, but Salem stayed at the house. Now we have three boats in the Gypsy Fleet, and it's because Delta took us into her home and her heart. Without her help, we might have ended up going from one odd job to another."

"You've all paid her back. You've given her companionship and you've cared about her all these years. I doubt she feels you owe her anything."

He wasn't sure he would have been as generous as Cass was under the circumstances. They had taken her place in Delta's life, yet she didn't appear to resent it.

"What about your life with Myra?" he asked. "From what little you've said, it doesn't sound like you had an easy time of it with her."

Cass shrugged. "Her drinking didn't become a serious problem until four or five years ago. Before that it was only the occasional binge. We used to travel a great deal, mostly in the summer when I was out of school, checking out various resorts for her agency. It was an exciting life."

Remembering what little he'd learned about Myra's drinking problem, he knew there was more she wasn't telling him. As he watched her, he realized it didn't matter. Whatever she'd gone through had made her the woman she was today.

He decided to take advantage of her willingness to talk more freely late at night. "There is one thing I can't help being curious about."

"What's that?"

"I realize in this enlightened age that women are quite capable of getting along without men, but there seems to me to be a distinct lack of men in all of your lives. Yours, Delta's, and Myra's. I know Delta was married once a long time ago, but she never talks about her husband. You've never mentioned anything about either Myra or yourself being involved with a man. You don't even seem interested in finding out who your father was."

"I know who he was."

By now, Wyatt thought, he should be used to her bombshell statements, but he wasn't. "That's why you told Delta it wasn't necessary for her to tell you about your father. You already knew."

She smiled at the note of indignation in his voice. "You're a real sucker for happy endings, aren't you? What did you expect when I came back? That Delta would be reunited with her long-lost daughter, make a sensible explanation, and all would be hunky-dory?"

"Would that be so dreadful?"

"Just unrealistic. Delta had an affair after her husband died. Her marriage hadn't been particularly happy. He wanted a full-time wife, not one who wanted a career, certainly not one who wanted to be an artist, of all things. When he died of a heart attack, she was finally free to do what she wanted. She was forty years old and grabbed at life with both hands to make up for lost time. She met a man who wasn't interested in being tied down any more than she was."

"Your father?"

"Biologically. A lot happened all at once. Delta found out she was pregnant right after she'd been accepted at an art school in Paris. Her lover took off as soon as he learned there would be a child. She waited until I was born, then dumped me on Myra before she flew off to Paris."

"Did I make a rash statement at one time about you not opening up to me? If I did, I take it all back. How did you learn all of this?"

"From Myra in bits and pieces. She tends to get very chatty after a few drinks. After a lot of drinks she gets maudlin and introspective, as well as chatty."

"She knew who your father was?"

"She should. He was her brother."

"Sweet heaven," he muttered.

Cass had rested her chin on her arms. When she finished, she bent her head until her forehead lay on her arms. It was impossible for him to see her face. Needing to have some sort of contact with her, he stroked her back. When his hand ran down her spine without encountering any interference, he realized she wasn't wearing anything under the thin cotton shirt. That discovery didn't help his heart one bit, but it certainly took his mind off the shock of her last blunt statement.

He slid his hand up to her shoulder and pressed her back against the couch. Slipping one arm around her, he shifted her until she was leaning against him, her head resting on his chest. Her lack of resistance was like a gift he hadn't expected. With her, he was learning to appreciate the smallest concession. A tiny step became a giant leap when she relinquished her cool control and accepted his right to touch her.

There was something he needed to clear up before he went any farther with her. "Cass?"

She sighed. "What?"

"Do you resent the fact that Delta took us in and left you out?"

"I don't resent you or John or Salem. I told you before. It wasn't your fault or theirs. It was a choice Delta made." She turned her head so she could see his face. "Is that what you wanted to know?"

Her lips were slightly parted, and he lowered his head to touch her moist mouth. "Yes. I don't want it between us."

She ran her tongue over her bottom lip to savor the taste of him, then her eyes widened as he groaned deep in his throat. Turning slightly, she laid her hand on his chest. "What's wrong?"

A corner of his mouth curved upward as he settled his hands at her waist. "Nothing's wrong." His grip tightened, and he lifted her across his thighs. "This is right. So right."

When his mouth covered hers, she twined her arms around his neck, holding him tightly as he kissed her hard, hungry, deep, hot. When he stroked her thigh, a sound of yearning came from her. He left a trail of fire as he caressed her hip, her belly. She jerked when she felt his hand settle between her legs.

Wyatt sucked in his breath when her thigh

brushed against the hard ridge beneath his jeans as she instinctively parted her legs. Bending his head, he buried his face in her neck, shudders of desire rocking through him.

He would find it easier to cut off his hand than move it from between her legs, especially when she was rolling her hips with a slow, sensual motion. Trying to hold on to his sanity, he muttered, "I want you so badly, I'm going crazy."

Cass couldn't stop the tremors of need exploding through her. "I want you too."

He raised his head to look into her eyes and almost lost the tentative hold on his control when he saw the glazed passion there. "But I didn't plan on making love to you when I came to the studio tonight, Cass. I can't protect you."

"It doesn't matter," she said, frustrated desire roughening her voice.

His smile was tender. "Yes, it does. We're the last people who should be irresponsible about birth control. We both know how painful it can be to be an unwanted child."

His words were like a bucket of ice water on a raging fire. The flames were extinguished, but hot embers still simmered. "I know you're right," she said, "but I hope you don't expect me to applaud your wisdom right now. Not when I'm aching like this."

Wyatt almost lost it. Knowing she was as aroused as he was gave him a high he'd never felt before. He allowed himself one last stroke over the part of her that was the center of her ache. Then he removed his hand, laying his arm across her thighs. He didn't trust himself to speak just then, not until he could control the overwhelming need to be inside her.

Cass withdrew her arms from around his neck and started to get off his lap, but he wouldn't allow it. Lifting her gaze to his, she said, "We should go in."

He shook his head. "Not yet. I can't let go of you yet. I need to hold you a little longer."

Keeping her close, he brought her down with him onto the cushions. He lay on his side with her facing him, her breasts pressed against his chest. He felt her warm breath flow over his skin as she began to relax.

Her breathing slowed and deepened as she fell asleep in his arms, but he didn't loosen his embrace. In an attempt to find a more comfortable position, she nudged her leg between his, bringing her thigh against his iron-hard manhood. Wyatt clenched his teeth as hot desire speared through him. But he didn't move her leg away.

It promised to be a long night, yet he wouldn't trade a good night's sleep for the delicious feel of her in his arms.

Six

Cass slowly opened her eyes the next morning and stretched out her arm to loosen her cramped muscles. Dropping her hand onto the pillow next to her, she felt something cool and soft. Puzzled, she turned her head and saw a sprig of bougainvillea lying on the pillow, the deep-red blossoms brilliant against the white case.

Picking up the small branch of flowers, she rolled onto her back. She was touched by the gesture Wyatt had made, although it wasn't one she would have expected from him, though perhaps she should have. Apparently she wasn't the only one who had hidden depths they didn't allow others to see.

Frowning slightly as she gazed up at the ceiling, she brushed the soft petals across her lips as she thought about how she'd gotten into this bed. She didn't remember being carried back to the bedroom, and that was disconcerting. The years of living with Myra had honed her senses so that she was aware of the slightest disturbance during the night. Usually she was a light sleeper, awake the instant she heard any sound out of the ordinary.

Another thought jolted her, and she lifted the sheet covering her. She wore only the white T-shirt and her panties. Good grief, she thought in astonishment. He'd removed her skirt, and she had slept right through it. The last thing she remembered was being held in his arms on the couch. There was a vague memory of his lips touching hers, but she could have been dreaming. Now she wasn't so sure.

She tossed back the sheet and swung her legs over the side of the bed. Instead of lying there mooning over a man, she'd be better off remembering why she had come to the island.

After taking a shower, she dressed in a pair of white shorts with thin blue stripes and a matching shirt. Slipping on a pair of leather sandals, she took the denim skirt she'd found folded on the dresser and returned it to the suitcase. It probably wouldn't make sense to anyone else, but living out of a suitcase reminded her she was there only temporarily. This wasn't her room. She was a guest. Nothing more, nothing less.

When she went into the kitchen, Connie insisted she eat something before she did anything else. Cass stared wide-eyed at the array of food Connie set in front of her. There was a baked apple, chipped beef gravy over a freshly baked biscuit, scrambled eggs, juice, and a cup of coffee.

"This isn't all for me, is it?" she asked hopefully as the housekeeper set a carafe of coffee on the table.

"Of course, child. The others have eaten."

"Could you have a cup of coffee and keep me company? This might take a while."

Connie nodded. "I'll get another cup."

Once the housekeeper was seated across the table, Cass picked up her fork and began to make inroads into the large breakfast.

She didn't know what was expected of her, so she decided to find out. "I know I can't spend a great deal of time with Delta because she needs her rest. Is there anything else she would like me to do now that I'm here?"

"I believe she mentioned she would like you to become acquainted with the gallery. She has also said you are to use the studio whenever you wish. If you need any supplies that aren't there, just make a list and they'll be provided."

Cass stared at the slice of apple on her fork. "I won't be using the studio."

"It was not an order, only a request," Connie said patiently. "You are welcome to accompany me when I go to the shops each morning. Also, I believe Mr. John would like you to visit Miss Salem when you can. She is nearing her time and you would help her by taking her mind away from her discomforts. They live several blocks away. It's within walking distance, but I can arrange for a ride if you prefer not to walk."

It looked as if she wouldn't have a problem with boredom while she was in Key West, Cass mused. She couldn't help noting that Connie had mentioned everyone except Wyatt. Apparently he was the only one who hadn't put in any requests for her time. Maybe it was just as well. It was going to be hard enough leaving the island at the end of two weeks, without the added complication of breaking off an intimate relationship.

"I need to make a long-distance phone call this morning," she said, "but I'll get the charges and pay for it."

Connie didn't argue over the matter. "There is a telephone in the library where you could have some privacy. Miss Delta wants you to feel at home here. Whatever you might need, you have only to ask."

"There is one thing," Cass said hesitantly. Meeting Connie's inquiring gaze, she asked, "How do you feel about having some of the flowers outside picked?"

"They are to be enjoyed both inside and out."

"Well, I have a sprig of bougainvillea I would like to put in a bud vase, if you have one,"

Connie didn't ask how Cass had acquired the flowers, other than to comment, "That explains why there was a knife in the sink this morning. Mr. Wyatt never was much for cleaning up after himself."

Cass had been in the process of taking a sip of coffee, and she had to stop when she started choking on the hot liquid. Connie calmly patted her on the back and smiled.

The next couple of days fell into a pattern of sorts. After breakfast Cass would spend time with Delta, go shopping with Connie, spend a couple of hours with Salem, then see Delta again. Dinner was on a tray in Delta's room, since there were no others dining with them. John didn't want Salem to tire herself out by walking over to Delta's house, and Salem refused to ride such a short distance.

Wyatt was taking over the fleet completely so that John could spend all of his time with his wife. Both men knew Salem didn't know the meaning of half measures. To her, taking it easy meant walking quickly instead of running flat out. The only time John left Salem alone was when Cass came over. Then he would run any errands he'd held off doing so that he could be with Salem.

It was John who explained to Cass, her second day in Key West, that Wyatt had taken a group out for a three-day charter. What surprised Cass more than Wyatt being away was John's manner when he told her, as though it was her right to know where Wyatt was.

On her fourth night on the island Cass left Delta's room a little before ten o'clock. The older woman was feeling the best she'd felt in a long time and had demonstrated how improved her health was by beating Cass at numerous games of gin rummy.

After showering, Cass fell into bed and stretched her tired body. In such a short time she had become enmeshed in Delta's life and the lives of those around her. She'd spent several hours at the gallery that afternoon helping the manager rehang some of the paintings. Then she'd visited Salem, which was taxing in a different way.

She smiled as she remembered the look on John's face when he had returned to the house to find them in the kitchen making English toffee. A simple batch of fudge was too easy for Salem. She wanted English toffee. In the spirit of trying to keep the pregnant woman occupied, Cass had gone along with the idea—then regretted it when she discovered exactly what making toffee entailed. She stirred the sugary syrup in a large caldron for what seemed like an hour while Salem sat at the kitchen table chopping nuts. With one eye on the bubbling mixture and one on Salem in case she sliced off a finger or two, Cass continued to stir, wondering where Salem got her energy and debating whether she should ask her for some.

By the time the chocolate was melted and spread over the cooling toffee, Cass was glad for the chance to sit down. She stayed seated while Salem sprinkled nuts over the chocolate, flipped the hardening toffee over onto wax paper, then spread more chocolate and nuts before exclaiming they were done. Cass could only stare open-mouthed when Salem proceeded to name various people who might like the toffee. Salem didn't like toffee. She'd just wanted to make some.

A light breeze ruffled the curtain at the open window, flowing lightly over her skin as she lay on top of the sheet. Whether it was the warm tropical temperatures or her own inner heat, she was thankful for any cool breeze nature could provide. In lieu of a nightgown she had slipped on a deep-purple chemise that ended at the top of her thighs. The spaghetti straps were so thin they were almost nonexistent. It was the skimpiest item of clothing in her limited wardrobe, and the coolest.

Her last thought as the edges of sleep claimed her was of a man with sun-streaked blond hair and sparkling blue eyes. It had been three days since she'd seen him. It seemed like forever.

*　　*　　*

The large grandfather clock in the hall was chiming midnight as Wyatt climbed the stairs, concentrating on each step. Lord, he was tired. Some charters were more difficult than others. This last one was a real pip. God save him from inept fishermen and women who never stopped talking.

He grabbed the railing when his deck shoe caught on the carpet of the stairs, and winced as his palm contacted the wood. It wasn't the first time a fish hook had been imbedded in his flesh, and it wouldn't have been so painful if the idiot holding the fishing rod hadn't tried to remove the hook by yanking his pole. It had taken two stitches at the emergency clinic to close the gash below his thumb. The only satisfaction he'd gotten out of the whole episode was putting the client's name down on the list of people they would never allow to book a charter with the Gypsy Fleet again.

It had been a long time since he'd taken out a fishing charter, and he'd forgotten how demanding some of the clients could be. If Charlie hadn't needed time to take care of some personal business, Wyatt wouldn't have taken the charter. Give him serious diving students over fledgling fishermen any day.

When he reached the door of his bedroom, he paused and glanced down the hallway to Cass's room. There was no sign of light around the closed door. At this hour she'd undoubtedly be asleep, unless she was taking another midnight stroll to the studio.

He dropped his hand away from the latch and walked to Cass's door. After the day he'd had, he needed to see her. Each time he'd talked to John on the boat's radio, he'd heard about Cass's visits to Salem. The knot of tension in his stomach eased whenever John merely mentioned her name. The first day out, he'd had to admit part of his tension was from wondering if she would up and leave while he was out at sea. He'd left before she had become adjusted to the situation between her and Delta, and he didn't know if she might fly back to Biloxi if she learned something that disturbed her.

Even though John said she was still there, he needed to see her. Now. Just to look at her, he promised himself. He hadn't seen her in three long, damnable days, and he wasn't going to go another minute without a glimpse of her.

As he swung her door open, the light from the hall fell across the foot of her bed. Like a curtain parting sideways, the light revealed Cass by tantalizing inches.

Wyatt's whole body became rigid as he gazed at her bare thighs, then the gentle slope of her bottom. She was lying on her side with her back to the door, in the middle of the double bed, one leg bent slightly under the other. The light reflected off the folds of the dark silky fabric covering her hips, her waist, her back. One delicate strap had slid down her shoulder.

He closed his eyes as desire rocked him. He had felt the need for a woman before, but nothing like this. Never like this, as though he would explode. And all he'd done was look at her.

When he opened his eyes again, he didn't trust

himself to look at her again until he'd caught his breath. His gaze fell on a bud vase sitting on the bureau against one wall. The small branch he'd cut off of the bougainvillea bushes near the house was in the vase. He smiled. It seemed his gift had been appreciated.

Unable to resist, he stepped into the room. As he shut the door, the swath of light reversed its path until there was no illumination except for the pale moonlight coming through the window. Like a moth attracted to a flame, he crossed the room. When he reached the side of the bed she was facing, he stopped and gazed down at her. Her scent reached out to him, feeding his senses with the fragrance of her hair, her skin, her own feminine essence.

He couldn't stop himself. He raised his hand and stroked the delicate curve of her shoulder. Her skin felt like the warm tropical sea flowing under his fingers.

She made a sound, a purr not a protest, as she moved her shoulder under his hand. He started to withdraw before he woke her, but she brought her other hand up and wrapped her fingers around his wrist, effectively stopping him from moving away. He heard his name on her lips, a husky murmur that sent shivers of awareness up his spine. He jerked his gaze to her face. Her eyes were closed, her breathing as deep and slow as before.

His heart thudded painfully in his chest when he realized she had reached for him in her sleep. And she knew who was touching her. It was his name she had whispered.

She didn't release him, and he suddenly felt an

aversion to prying her fingers loose. Instead of leaving, which would be the sensible thing to do, he sank down on the edge of the bed, finding the symbolism of his inability to let go of her hand appropriate.

He didn't think he was ever going to be able to let go of Cassandra Mason.

Cass slowly opened her eyes. She knew instantly who the shadowy figure was sitting next to her, even though she couldn't see his features clearly. He had brought the scent of salt water, fresh air, and sunshine into the room. She didn't know what time it was or why he had come to her room, but it didn't matter. The important thing was he was there.

"Hi," she said, her voice husky with sleep,

"Hi," he murmured. "I'm sorry. I didn't mean to wake you." He didn't tell her he'd had to make sure she was still there, trusting only his own eyes rather than what John had told him.

Her fingers tightened on his. "It doesn't matter." The way he held himself gave her the impression he was tired. His normally straight back was bowed slightly, as if his shoulders were carrying a heavy burden.

"Rough day?" she asked.

He brought his free hand up to her head, his touch light as he let several fingers thread through her tousled hair. "I've had better."

She tugged on the hand she still held. He accepted the wordless invitation and stretched out beside her on his back. Sighing heavily, he brought their clasped hands up to rest on his chest and enclosed them with his other hand.

One minute she was lying quietly beside him, then she was rolling over on top of him to reach for the small lamp on the bedside stand. Propping herself up on an elbow, she grabbed his hand.

She stared down at the white gauze wrapped around his palm and part of his thumb, then raised her gaze to his. Her eyes flashed with anger at his hurt. "What happened?"

He blinked, more against her sudden ferocity than the flare of light. "One of our customers got a little confused as to what he was fishing for. He hooked me instead of a fish."

She relaxed and smiled. "According to Salem, you're considered quite a catch."

"She also thinks every day is Christmas. How is she feeling? All I got from John on the radio was a grunt or two."

Cass described the last visit with Salem, pleased when he chuckled over the candy-making episode. She could feel his body relax against her, and proceeded to tell him about some of the things she'd been doing the last couple of days, her voice low and intimate.

He watched her the whole time. When she finished, she examined his face carefully. "You should get some sleep, Wyatt. You look like you haven't had a decent night's rest in days."

"I haven't."

His gaze lowered to the front of the chemise she wore. Because of the way she was lying, the material was pulled tightly across her breasts, part of the fabric caught under her body. The other strap had slipped down her arm, too, allowing the silky fabric to fall lower, exposing the slope of her breast. He shifted so that he could lie on his side facing her. Lowering his head, he touched his lips to the gentle swell of her breasts. He smiled when he heard her shuddering breath.

"I know," he murmured. "This isn't going to help either one of us get some sleep, but who needs sleep?"

Her fingers twined through his hair. "You do."

"I need this more."

His mouth closed over the tip of her breast through the silk. The material became wet, his mouth hot, the combination creating a flood of heat along her veins. He tugged the chemise down to expose her breasts. She cried out softly when she felt his lips close over her bare skin, finally taking her taut nipple into his mouth.

She stroked her hand over his jean-clad hip from his waistband to his thigh, then back again. Sliding her hand into the back pocket, she pulled him toward her. He made a sound of tormented pleasure when his hard arousal was against her soft body.

He released her breast only to claim her lips. He took her mouth with all the hunger that had built up in him over the last three days. She took him in, her tongue stroking his, her taste exploding through him. Her response overwhelmed him, made his head spin, his blood thicken, his breath drag in and out of his lungs.

He stroked his hand over her hot, satiny skin, caressing her stomach, then lower.

She arched her back, pressing against his

hand. She was hot and moist, driving him crazy with the need to be inside her.

When he felt her fingers fumbling with the snap of his jeans, reality came crashing down around him. Raising his head, he cursed softly and bluntly as he brought his hand up to stop her.

"No," he said in a rasping, hoarse voice.

For a moment Cass couldn't move, frozen by the word and what it meant. She slowly tugged her hand until he released it. Concentrating on what she was doing, she pulled the straps of the chemise up to her shoulders and adjusted the neckline. It wasn't enough. She still felt naked and exposed, her nerve endings raw and bleeding.

Clutching the sheet to her breast, she rolled away from him. Even if she could have thought of something to say, she wouldn't have been able to get the words out of her tight throat.

Her body jerked when he touched her shoulder, then relief flowed through her when he removed his hand. The relief was short-lived.

In one swift motion he turned her onto her back and leaned over her. "Dammit, Cass. I was almost at the point of no return. One second more of feeling you rubbing against me, and I would have been inside you."

He saw the spark of desire ignite again in her eyes as she stared up at him. Then the hurt crowded it out until it disappeared. Taking a deep breath, he forced himself to concentrate on what he had to say. "Cass, I'm no better prepared than I was the other night in the studio. I want you more than my next breath, but I can't take the chance of making you pregnant."

Still clutching the sheet in a knot at her breast, she murmured, "I understand."

He stared down at her, seeing the humiliation in her eyes until she lowered her lashes, shutting him out. Angry with himself for handling this so badly, he swore under his breath.

"I would like you to leave now," she said, her expression blank, her voice cool and self-contained. "Please. I'm very tired."

"We need to talk about this, dammit."

"Not now," she muttered, a hint of desperation entering her voice. She raised her eyes to his, her gaze direct and unflinching. "I'm tired and so are you. We're liable to say things that would only make matters worse."

He couldn't imagine how they could get much worse, but maybe she was right. His body still throbbed with wanting her, his brain was muddled as though it were wrapped in cotton, and his hand hurt. What he needed was several hours of sleep, and then he would be able to think straight and make some sort of sense.

"All right. We'll talk tomorrow," he promised as he levered himself off the bed. He reached over and shut off the lamp, then walked toward the door in the dark. As he opened it, the light from the hall fell across her face.

"Cass, will you promise me something?"

She didn't say anything, and he went on. "Don't leave the island because of me, because of this."

She raised her arm and laid it across her eyes, blocking out the light from the hall. "I won't leave because of you," she said so quietly he had to strain to hear her.

It wasn't until he was stripping off his clothes in the next room that he realized she hadn't promised not to leave the island, just not to leave because of him.

Seven

Cass didn't have to worry how she would react when she saw Wyatt again. At least not for a while. He was gone to the marina by the time she came downstairs the next morning. She had the whole day to regain her equilibrium before seeing him again. Maybe it would be long enough.

She would have liked more time, but it was all she was going to get. According to Delta, Wyatt would be there in the evening for dinner. So would John and Salem, if Salem felt up to it. It was to be a celebration of sorts. The doctor was so pleased with Delta's progress he was allowing her to come downstairs for dinner, so long as someone brought her down, rather than having her navigate the two flights of stairs on her own. She no longer needed to be hooked up to the oxygen tank and was feeling better than she had for a long time.

Since John had told Salem she'd have to rest all afternoon if she wanted to go to Delta's for dinner, Cass was at loose ends until she went to the gallery to see if she could help the manager, who was suffering from a sinus headache and was more than pleased to accept Cass's offer to handle the customers.

For several hours in the early afternoon, business generally picked up, when many of the tourists wisely took advantage of the shops instead of exposing themselves to the tropical sun during the hottest part of the day. The hour before closing was slower, with few people browsing through the gallery. During that lull Cass strolled around the gallery, examining each painting closely, especially the ones Delta had painted. Delta's paintings did reveal more about the woman than anything Delta had said during Cass's visits to her room. Technically Delta's brushstrokes and composition couldn't be faulted by the most discerning eye. But it was the way she used color that made her style so unique, so compelling. Cass felt sensitivity and emotion in each stroke, two feelings she wouldn't have associated with the artist before she'd become reacquainted with her.

She was still no closer to finding out why Delta had traded her role as a mother for that of an artist. The two could have been combined, could even have complemented each other. Women made these compromises all the time. The fact that Delta had taken John, Salem, and Wyatt into her home and into her heart proved the older woman could mix the responsibilities of her career with caring for other people. Noting the dates on the labels of some of Delta's paintings, Cass thought the artist's best work had been done while the three younger people had lived with her. She wondered if Delta was aware of that.

Even though Cass had spent a great deal of time with Delta over the last several days, they had never touched on their personal feelings or motivations. Most of the conversations were about Myra's progress at the clinic, which Cass checked every day by phone, or answering Delta's questions about Cass's work at Filmer's Fancy Fudge, the places she'd traveled with Myra, everything but the subject of Delta's abandonment. Often the conversation revolved around Delta's artwork. Her painting was the central force of her life, her way of communicating. It was obvious she sorely missed being able to paint since her illness.

That morning Cass had taken a sketch pad and some pastel pencils to Delta's room. The glow of pleasure in Delta's eyes was more than enough reward for bringing her the art supplies.

The only moments of tension between the two women came when Delta asked Cass when she was going to use the studio. Connie had reported to her that Cass hadn't done so, and Delta had pushed several times for Cass to paint while she was on the island. It was obvious Delta was disappointed. She wanted to see how Cass's technique had developed over the years. Several times she reminded Cass that if she didn't get a painting started soon, there wouldn't be time for her to complete it before she left the island. Without explaining why, Cass told her she painted only for the ads she did. Delta had given her a long look, then changed the subject.

Aside from the subject of Cass using the studio,

each visit with Delta was easier, but vaguely unsatisfying, and Cass was no closer to getting the answers she needed before she returned to Biloxi. It was just possible she might never get them. The longer she knew Delta, the less she wanted to upset the tentative relationship they had begun to build.

Knowing where she came from wasn't as important as knowing where she was going, she decided as she walked home from the gallery a little after five o'clock. She had survived for twenty-seven years without fully understanding the circumstances that had led to her living with a woman who existed mainly to have her next drink, instead of the woman who lived for her art.

When Cass entered the kitchen, Connie informed her that Delta was following doctor's orders by resting before coming downstairs for dinner. Cass frowned when she heard the news. "I hope she isn't coming down just because I'm here. I don't want to be the reason she has a relapse."

"It's what she wants to do," Connie assured her, "to prove to everyone, and mostly to herself, she's getting better."

Watching the housekeeper's graceful movements as she reached into one of the cupboards, Cass said, "I knew she'd been ill before I came. I don't expect to be entertained."

Holding a cookie tin in her hands, Connie looked at her directly. "What did you expect, child?"

"Answers."

"And have you found them?"

Cass shook her head. "Not all of them. Maybe I never will."

Connie smiled. "Not all things in life require clear-cut answers and explanations."

Thinking of Wyatt, Cass agreed. "Sometimes they just cause more questions."

As Connie placed freshly baked cookies from the cooling rack into the square tin, she asked Cass if she would mind cleaning up the studio for Delta.

"Now that she's being allowed to come down for dinner, the next thing she'll badger the doctor for is permission to paint. I would consider it a great favor if you would tidy up the studio. I fear Delta would take one look and start mopping and dusting the minute she walked in the door. Even if she isn't able to go there anytime soon, it will make her feel as though everything is ready for her."

"I don't mind cleaning the studio," Cass said, reaching for one of the fragrant cookies still on the rack. "I'll start on it in the morning."

Connie shook her head in exasperation as Cass bit down into the cookie. "You will spoil your dinner, Miss Cassandra. You are as bad as Mr. Wyatt. He just came through here and took a handful of cookies up to his room with him."

Rather than chance running into Wyatt just yet, Cass grabbed another cookie, ducking away from Connie's hand. "I'm going out to the studio to get an idea what needs to be done."

"Don't be too long. Dinner is in an hour."

"I won't be late."

Outside, she followed the path to the studio. Once there, she only gave the room a cursory look, then walked over to the couch. Curling her legs under her, she simply sat there, watching

the dust motes float in the air as the fading sunlight shone through the skylights. She had no
way of knowing what Wyatt's reaction was going
to be when she saw him again. She didn't know
him well enough to be able to predict his mood.

That was part of the problem, at least for her.
They didn't really know each other very well. Yet
the physical attraction between them seemed natural and right. Wyatt had been the one to put
an end to their lovemaking before it reached its
natural conclusion. She should be glad he wasn't
allowing their relationship to become more intimate. He wanted her, but evidently not enough
to have an affair with a woman who was only
going to be there for a short time.

He'd rejected her twice. She had to make sure
there wouldn't be a third time.

Her gaze settled on a solitary paintbrush lying
on the rough-plank coffee table in front of the
couch. After staring at it for several minutes, she
bent forward and picked it up. She ran her forefinger over the soft bristles, feeling a resurgence
of the desire to dip a brush into paint and let her
pent-up emotions explode on a canvas. Soon she
was going to have to face Wyatt, and she needed
an outlet for the tensions within her that left her
feeling as strung out as a tight clothesline.

Uncurling her legs, she got up off the couch
and walked over to the stack of blank stretched
canvases. Choosing a medium-sized one, she carried it over to the easel. After removing the partially finished painting of herself, she set the
blank canvas on the easel. Stepping back three
paces, she tightly gripped the brush and stared
at the stark white surface.

It was silly how nervous she was at the thought of painting again, she mused as she continued to study the canvas. The vow she'd made when she was seventeen never to paint again had been an act of defiance that seemed ridiculous now. It was as though she had blamed painting for the past, rather than the person who was the painter. She knew now that she'd been afraid painting would take over her life to the exclusion of everything and everyone else. Like she thought it had for Delta.

For over ten years she'd suppressed her desire to paint, but it had always been there just under the surface, like an itch she wouldn't allow herself to scratch.

Her attention was so focused on the canvas, she didn't hear the door open behind her. Wyatt had come to tell her dinner was about to be served, but when he saw her standing in front of the easel, he remained silent. Something about the way she held herself kept him from interrupting her. She reminded him of a tightrope walker about to take a dangerous walk across the thin line, unsure whether to take that first step or not.

When she lowered her hand, he could see the long brush she held tightly. Shifting his gaze to the tall table near the easel, he noticed she hadn't squeezed any fresh paint out of the tubes. But she had put a blank canvas on the easel.

She'd taken the first step after all.

Without fully understanding why, he felt pained watching her stare at the canvas without making any move to paint. He could see her fingers flexing around the brush. He wanted to say something, anything to help her over the hurdle that prevented her from taking the final step of applying paint to the canvas.

When five minutes passed and neither had moved, Wyatt stepped back and closed the door quietly behind him. Someone else was going to have to interrupt Cass and tell her dinner was ready. It wasn't going to be him.

He frowned as he pushed one of the low-hanging tree limbs out of his way as he walked back to the house. After last night Cass might not want anything from him, even a simple invitation to dinner.

Connie was serving the first course when Cass entered the dining room. She hadn't realized it was so late. Meeting Delta's gaze from the opposite end of the table, she apologized for being late. "I guess time got away from me."

Delta nodded. "I understand perfectly. I have often lost track of time when I've been in the studio."

Pulling out her chair, Cass sat down and kept her gaze on her napkin as she unfolded it. She didn't know whether it would be kinder to tell Delta the truth, that she hadn't been painting, or to let her think she'd finally begun again. She did neither. Thankfully, no one else at the table thought it strange she had been in the studio. Except perhaps Wyatt. She could feel his gaze on her, but she wouldn't look at him.

In fact she didn't once look in his direction while she pretended to eat the food Connie put in front of her. If that made her a coward, then that's what she was. She wasn't ready to see a blank look on his face, as though he had put last night completely out of his mind, marking it off as one of those things that happen and are better forgotten. She couldn't forget the time she'd spent in his arms or the melting way she responded to his kisses, the touch of his hands, the delicious feel of his hard body against hers.

Nor did she want to see regret in his eyes. She didn't want him to wish those moments between them hadn't happened, even if the evening hadn't ended the way either of them wanted.

And he had wanted her, she knew. Which was why she found it difficult to understand why he'd rejected her. Again.

The meal was more of a sumptuous feast than a simple dinner. Connie had prepared conch chowder, two kinds of fish, steamed shrimp, several vegetables and salads, and ended the meal with Key lime pie and coffee. It was a shame no one did justice to the food. Salem was obviously uncomfortable with her advanced state of pregnancy, adjusting her position on the chair enough times to cause John to keep his attention on her rather than his dinner. Delta was more interested in the people at the table. Wyatt spent more time twirling his wineglass around and around than he did using his fork.

Delta was nearing her deadline for the amount of time the doctor was allowing her to be out of bed, when she turned to Wyatt. "I can see John is checking his watch every few minutes. Since he isn't timing Salem's contractions yet, he must be counting the minutes I have left before he takes me back upstairs to my room. Before he does that, I have a favor to ask."

Wyatt glanced briefly at Cass, not at all surprised she wasn't looking at him. The last favor

Delta had asked of him had caused him a lot of sleepless nights. He wasn't sure he could take doing another one.

"Just name it," he said, resigned.

"Cassandra hasn't had a chance to see much of the island or to take advantage of the fact that she knows the owners of the Gypsy Fleet. I was hoping you could take her out on one of the boats. John said the charters are all covered for tomorrow, so you wouldn't be needed to take any of them out. He also said the *Gypsy II* would be available if you wanted to take it."

Wyatt didn't comment that John must have had to do some fancy maneuvering with the schedule. When he'd checked the logbook earlier in the day, Wyatt had noted that every boat was booked solid for two weeks. Instead of debating the issue, he nodded. "No problem. If Cass wants to go, I'll take her, but I think you should ask her first."

Before Delta could do so, Cass placed her napkin on the table and pushed back her chair. Meeting Wyatt's gaze for the first time that night, she said, "Could we discuss this in private?" Without waiting for his answer, she marched out of the dining room toward the front door.

Wyatt blinked, then recovered swiftly. Tossing his napkin on the table, he mumbled, "Excuse me."

The remaining members of the dining party looked from one to the other for a few seconds before they all started grinning.

Giggling, Salem looked at her husband with laughing eyes. "Do you think we should tell them about the banyan tree?" Ignoring John's choked laugh, she went on to explain, "It's a great place to work out tensions."

Before she could go into detail about the time he'd made love to her under the banyan tree at the side of the house, or more truthfully, against the trunk of the banyan tree, John said, "Poor Wyatt. He doesn't stand a chance with all you women plotting behind his back. After you called me, Delta, I had to do some fancy talking to get a couple to postpone their fishing trip for a couple of days so that the *Gypsy II* would be available. The only way they would agree was if I gave them the charter at half price."

Unabashed, Delta faced him. "I didn't hear any complaints about our meddling when you and Salem were being real dunderheads about how you felt about each other. Lord knows, it wasn't all smooth sailing between you two until we finally managed to knock some sense into you."

"I thought the Porto brothers were the ones who did that," John said, "when they tried to take over the fleet." He raised both hands palms out in a gesture of surrender. "Never mind. Leave me with a few illusions. I don't want to know."

Sitting back in her chair, Delta smiled smugly. "We weren't going to tell you anyway. You might as well take me to my room now, John. It's doubtful we will see any more of those two tonight."

Wyatt followed Cass as she strode across the porch and down the front steps. He was only a step behind her when she stopped beside his Jeep parked in the driveway. He hadn't planned on leaving just yet, but apparently that was what she had in mind.

He was reminded of another night not too long ago when he'd been in the same position, leaning against the fender of a car waiting to hear what she had to say. "We seem to have a tendency to hold conversations in parking lots," he said.

"This way you can make a quick getaway."

Crossing his arms over his chest, he asked quietly, "Why would I want to do that?"

"I've noticed you have a tendency to when things start getting complicated."

Her voice was light and casual, but he could sense her tension. And her hurt. "I didn't stop making love to you because I wanted to, Cass. Either time. You know it was the sensible thing to do under the circumstances."

This time her voice had a bite in it that she couldn't conceal. "By all means, let's be sensible."

His eyes narrowed as he watched her, and he wished he could see her face more clearly, especially her eyes. She could hide a lot behind that cool expression she had perfected over the years, but not in her eyes. The light from the street lamp in front of Delta's house was adequate enough to keep them from stumbling around in the dark, but that was about all it was good for. The only way he was going to find out what she was thinking was to ask her and hope she would tell him.

"Do you have a problem with going out in a boat with me, or is it the fact that it was Delta's idea and not mine?"

"You don't have to take me anywhere. That's what I wanted to talk to you about. Delta means well, but she doesn't understand how things are between us."

He crossed one leg over the other at the ankle and studied her carefully. "How are things between us? I'd like to hear your views, since I sure as hell don't know."

"You should," she said with some irritation. "You're the one who's made the rules."

"What rules?" he asked, completely mystified. "I don't remember making any rules."

Now he was making her darned mad, Cass thought, and she'd wanted to be cool and matter-of-fact about this. Her pride insisted on it. "Forget it. Forget last night. Forget about tomorrow. I'll talk to her in the morning and let you off the hook."

"I don't need you to make excuses for me, Cass. With Delta or anyone else. Tell me the real reason you don't want to spend the day with me tomorrow. Are you afraid I'll attack your body again?"

No, she wanted to scream at him. She was afraid he wouldn't. She couldn't take another rejection from him, so she wasn't going to put herself in the position where she might have to. The anger she heard in his voice surprised her, although his stance was still relaxed and casual as he leaned against the Jeep.

Trying to sound logical and calm, she said, "You don't need to waste your time entertaining me. That wasn't part of the deal. I said I would come to the island for two weeks, and that's how long I'll stay. I came to spend time with Delta, to get to know her. That's the only reason I'm here."

"What about us?"

"There is no us, Wyatt. You've made that clear.

It's just a case of physical attraction that you've decided you don't want any part of. I was simply a little slow in understanding that."

In a sudden move he shoved away from the Jeep and wrapped his fingers around her wrist. She could feel his bandaged hand at the back of her neck as he pulled her toward him. He kissed her hard, then raised his head and growled, "You don't understand a damn thing."

The next minute Cass was sitting in the front seat of the Jeep and he was backing out of the driveway. She didn't bother asking where they were going. She doubted very much if he would tell her. His jaw was clenched, his fingers tight on the wheel as he sped away from the house. She didn't know why he was so angry, but she wasn't going to ask about that either. There weren't that many choices of where he would be taking her. The marina was a possibility, or his cottage. Or the airport.

He brought the Jeep to a screeching halt in the driveway of a cottage she'd never seen before. She couldn't really see much except for a shadowy outline against the lighter dark sky. There were no lights on inside, outside, or anywhere nearby. There could be houses on either side, but if there were, they were hidden by the trees and shrubbery.

Wyatt stalked around the front of the Jeep and yanked open her door. Without giving her a chance to refuse, he took her hand and practically pulled her off the seat until she was standing beside him. He started to draw her along with him, but she tripped over a clump of grass in the sidewalk and would have fallen if he hadn't tightened his hold on her hand.

"I can't see where I'm walking, Wyatt," she said in a reasonable voice. "Could you slow down?"

He stopped abruptly, and she almost ran into him. Looking down at her, he said tightly, "Do us both a favor, Cass. Don't say a word until we get inside. Okay? I just might be able to keep from strangling you until then."

She started to ask him why he was so angry, but decided it might be wiser to wait. She would soon find out once they were inside his house.

After giving her a long, hard look, he led her up the walk to the cottage. She stood quietly beside him as he slid a key into the lock and shoved the door open. He waited for her to precede him. She had taken three cautious steps into the pitch-black interior before he flicked a light switch near the front door.

He brushed past her, heading for the kitchen. "I'm going to make a pot of coffee. I know you don't drink it, but I need it."

Unsure what she was supposed to do, Cass glanced around the living room. The furniture was an eclectic mix of chairs, a couch, two end tables, and a large coffee table. She couldn't help smiling fleetingly at the sight of the clutter spread throughout the room. His windbreaker was thrown over the back of a chair. A number of empty white cardboard cartons from a Chinese take-out littered the coffee table, which had been made from a slab of a cypress tree. Next to a tilting stack of fishing magazines were three empty coffee cups. There was also a tin she recognized as coming from Connie's kitchen, indicating

Wyatt had helped himself to some of the house-keeper's cookie supply.

It didn't take much brilliance to deduct that Wyatt Brodie was not a neat person.

She was studying some of the framed certifi-cates and photos on the near wall, when he came out of the kitchen carrying a steaming cup of cof-fee. "Would you like something?" he asked as he sat on the arm of one of the chairs. "I don't have any milk, but there's a jug of iced tea and some orange juice."

She shook her head and stayed where she was. "Nothing, thanks. Why am I here, Wyatt?"

"It's time to get a few things straightened out between us without any interruptions." He saw the way she stiffened and wrapped her arms around her waist defensively. "Why don't you sit down and relax? Since getting you to talk about yourself and your feelings is like trying to pry open a giant clamshell, this might take a while."

She didn't sit down. He didn't seem as angry as he had been earlier, but she was still too wary to relax her guard. "If you're angry because Delta came down for dinner, it was her idea and okayed by her doctor. It had nothing to do with my being there. Connie said she needed to prove to every-one and herself that she was getting better."

"I'm not angry because Delta is well enough to come downstairs to dinner. Why would I be? She's recovering better than anyone expected, and it's partly because you're here."

Her eyes widened in surprise at his offhand compliment. "A minute ago you wanted to stran-gle me, and now you're patting me on the back. I don't get it."

He lowered his cup after taking a long swallow of coffee. "I can see we're going to have to use the interrogation technique again. It seems to be the only way I can get answers from you."

She was getting more confused by the minute. "What is this all about, then? If this is about last night when you came to my room, forget it. I have."

"I don't want you to forget it."

She took a deep breath to try to calm her agitation. "Then, what is it you want from me?" she asked with forced patience.

He slid off the arm of the chair and walked over to her. Ignoring the way she stepped backward to get away from him, he took her arm and led her over to the couch. Once she was seated, he sat down beside her, setting his cup on the coffee table before reaching for her. With his hands on her waist, he lifted her onto his lap.

Keeping one arm around her, he lay the other across her thighs. "I want you to understand why I left your bedroom last night when I did. No," he said when she lowered her eyes. "Look at me." He didn't continue until she'd done as he ordered. Holding her gaze with his own, he went on. "I have the distinct feeling you've concocted some muddleheaded explanation that has nothing to do with the real reason. I stopped making love to you because I didn't have any way of protecting you. Contrary to some women's beliefs, most men don't go around carrying condoms in their back pockets on the off chance they'll run into a willing woman. On a date maybe, but not when he's just come back from a three-day fishing trip with a bunch of guys and one married woman who talked so much even the sea gulls avoided us."

He was doing it again, Cass thought in amazement. He was the only person who could make her laugh at him and herself at the darndest times. "I know that's what you said, but I thought it might have something to do with who I am and why I was here."

It was his turn to look bewildered. "Cass, who you are has nothing to do with my wanting you, except for being the person that you are. If you mean you're worried I might think less of you because you've had an unusual childhood, I'd like to point out that mine isn't exactly out of *Leave It to Beaver* either. I don't give a damn who your parents are. Hell, I don't even remember what mine looked like. Maybe I should be asking you if that makes a difference to you."

"You know better than that."

"You should too." He bent his head and touched her lips. When he straightened, he smiled down at her. "Before we go any farther, perhaps I should point out that the reason I didn't make love to you last night is not going to be a problem tonight."

She could feel the rise and fall of his chest under her hand. His heart was racing. Her hip pressed against the front of his jeans, and she had no doubt of his reaction to her sitting on his lap.

She arched her neck when he began to nuzzle the soft, sensitive skin under her ear. "Wyatt?"

He sighed and raised his head so that he could see her face. "There's more?"

"I'm only going to be here for another ten days.

Are you sure you want to get involved with me, knowing I'm going to be leaving?"

Something flickered in his eyes, but it was gone before she could figure out what it was. "I've been involved with you since I saw you serving drinks in Biloxi. If all we have is ten days, then we shouldn't waste any more time."

Sliding one arm under her knees, he got up from the couch with her in his arms, lifting her effortlessly. After taking three steps toward his bedroom, he stopped and looked down at her, desire sharpening his gaze. "Are you sure this is what you want, Cass? Once I make love to you, there's no turning back. We can't be just friends after I've had you."

Her arms went around his neck, and she buried her face against his skin. "I want you. That's all I know."

His arms tightened around her. "That's enough for now."

Eight

When he reached his bed, Wyatt released her so that she was standing in front of him. With his hands at her waist, he could feel her tension. He knew how independent she was and could understand how difficult it was for her to relinquish some of her control to him. The fact that she was trusting him enough to give herself to him was mind-blowing.

The light from the lamp in the living room trickled through the doorway, giving enough illumination so that he could see her eyes and the expression in them. For a long time he simply looked at her, dazed by the glow of desire in her green eyes. Desire for him.

He didn't think he could want her any more than he had before. He was wrong. He felt a rush of primitive male exultation at the realization she wanted him as badly as he wanted her.

Raising his hand, he let the back of one finger glide over her cheek, her throat, the curve of her breast, stopping at the row of buttons down the front of her sundress. Slowly he released each button, his eyes never leaving hers as the bodice opened, allowing his hands inside.

He felt cool silk covering hot flesh. Parting the soft cotton, he lowered his gaze. She was wearing a chemise similar to the purple one she'd been sleeping in the night before. Sliding the dress off her arms, he ignored it as it fell in a heap on the floor.

He swept his hands over her, enjoying the feel of her under the slippery cool material. "How many of these things do you have?" he asked in a raw voice.

"I brought three with me." She lifted her hands to the front of his shirt. "Why?"

"Remind me to send whoever designed them a thank-you note."

Smiling, she unbuttoned his shirt. The apprehension she'd felt a moment earlier faded away, replaced by anticipation and an aching need to get as close to him as possible. "I'm glad you like them."

"Oh, I do." His fingers smoothed over her shoulders, taking each strap with them as they moved down her arm. "It's almost a shame to take this off you."

She pushed his shirt off. "But you will."

He shuddered as she stroked his bare skin. "Definitely."

The silk made a soft sound as it slid over her breasts, then her hips, until it landed on the floor. His heart pounded painfully, his blood heated. His fantasies had never even come close to the real thing. She was beautiful, more beautiful than he ever imagined a woman could be.

The tips of her breasts hardened as he gazed at her, and he reached for her, needing to feel her against his skin. Lowering his head, he took her mouth, open and hard, his tongue searching for hers. Her response was everything he could have asked for and more. She gave and took, she shared, holding nothing back, meeting him honestly, passionately.

His hands became restless as they passed over her feminine curves, until he'd driven himself nearly mad with the feel of her heated skin, her womanly shape. Breaking his mouth away from hers, he buried his lips against her neck, his body shuddering with the impact of his explosive need to make her his. He tried to slow himself down, to make it last, but his control slipped when she raised herself up on her toes, sliding her thighs against his.

She was burning him alive, and only she could put out the flames.

He lowered her to the bed and followed her down. "I need you now, Cass." He wanted to tell her he would need her forever, but he didn't. "I can't wait any longer or I'll explode."

Her fingers fumbled with the snap of his jeans. She met his hot gaze. "Don't wait."

He helped her slide his jeans and briefs down his legs, hearing her quick intake of breath when his bare flesh covered hers. Threading his fingers through one of her hands, he held on to her as he reached into the drawer of his bedside table with his free hand. A moment later he returned to her. Locking his gaze with hers, he laced his fingers with her other hand and lifted their clasped hands to either side of her head.

He paused at the threshold of her body when she spoke softly. "What's my name, Wyatt?"

The question penetrated his passion-fogged mind. He saw the vulnerability in her eyes and understood that she needed to know *he* knew whom he was going to claim.

"Cass," he said as he bent his head to kiss her. "Cassandra," he murmured against her mouth, pushing slowly into her. "Love," he groaned as he buried himself in her.

Sometime during the night, Cass opened her eyes. She didn't know what woke her. The room was dark. There were no sounds other than the soft, slow breathing of the man beside her. Wyatt's arm lay possessively across her waist, his body warm and firm against her side.

Apparently he had turned off the lamp in the living room at some point, since she could barely see anything but vague shadows. But she could feel. She lay absolutely still, afraid the delicious, languid sensation would disappear if she moved. She wanted to hold on to it for as long as she could, in case it never came back. Whatever happened in the future, she would have this memory of belonging to Wyatt, if only for a brief time.

The first sign she had that he was no longer asleep was when he cupped his hand around her side and drew her toward him. He sighed when her breasts brushed his chest.

His hand slid to her back, tracing the flowing

line of her spine. "What are you thinking?" he asked, his voice drowsy with sleep.

Whether it was the intimate curtain of darkness or the aftermath of his lovemaking, she found herself answering him honestly. "I was thinking I've never felt like this before. I was hanging on to the sensations so that I would remember them."

"Any regrets?"

How could she possibly regret taking a trip to paradise in his arms, she wondered as she traced his mouth with her finger. "None."

He didn't realize he'd been holding his breath for her answer until he let it out. "Good." He slipped his arm under her shoulders to hold her more firmly against him, making a sound deep in his throat. "You feel so good, green eyes. So good. It's okay to go back to sleep if you want to. The feelings will still be there in the morning. They aren't going anywhere, and neither are you."

She touched the gold medallion he wore. "I should go back to Delta's," she murmured without much conviction.

He lifted her over him, holding her hips between his firm hands as her slender body covered him. "No, you shouldn't. You should stay here, where you belong."

She could feel him rock hard against the junction of her thighs. Her fingers dug into his shoulders as she moved her hips in an undulating motion. Pleasure splintered through her as she reveled in the knowledge that she could make him respond to her. Lowering her head, she claimed his mouth, feeling the feminine power of being desired.

His hands tightened on her hips, guiding her, inciting himself. His breathing was ragged, his body rigid, but he managed to reach for the drawer of the bedside table. A few seconds later he met her gaze. "I'd better warn you now. I'm going to fight to keep you here, Cass."

She wasn't given a chance to argue with him. He was lifting his hips into hers, inviting her to take him.

The sun was just beginning to lighten the sky when the phone beside the bed rang. Wyatt reached for it, answering in his usual blunt fashion. "Brodie."

Ten seconds later he said, "We'll be right there."

As he tossed back the sheet, he glanced at Cass. Seeing she was awake, he ordered, "Get dressed, Cass. We've got to go to the hospital."

Fear sliced through her. "Is it Delta?"

Tugging on his jeans, he grinned at her. "It's Salem." He picked her dress up off the floor and tossed it in her direction. "You've got time for a quick shower while I make a pot of coffee. Then we've got to go prop John up. He sounded pretty shaky."

Cass attempted to untangle her legs from the sheet. "Why don't you go ahead without me? I'll just hold you up. You should be there with them as soon as you can."

Tearing a shirt off a hanger, he slipped his arms into it as he crossed the room to the bed. Even after the incredible intimacy they had shared, she apparently still felt like an outsider. He grabbed her arms and brought her up onto her knees on the mattress. He kissed her, then said, "I'm not going without you."

She started to open her mouth to try again, but he cut her off. "The more you argue, the longer it will be before we can get there." He drew her off the bed and marched her toward the bathroom. "Hurry up, Auntie Cass. Knowing Salem, she'll have the doctors, nurses, and even the janitors jumping to her command. I don't want to miss it."

When they arrived at the hospital, Cass finally managed to take a deep breath. Salem wasn't the only one who could churn up a whirlwind just by entering a room. Wyatt had whisked her out of the house the minute she left the bathroom, carrying her sandals for her, which she struggled into while he backed the Jeep out of his driveway.

John was in with Salem when they reached the waiting room. She had expected to see Connie there, but Delta was also present, sitting in a wheelchair. Wyatt strode up to the nurse's station and asked about Salem, then disappeared down the hall with one of the nurses.

Delta motioned for her to sit down. "It could be hours yet."

"How's John holding up?" Cass asked as she took the chair near Delta. "Wyatt said he sounded somewhat shaky on the phone."

The older woman chuckled. "He was holding up pretty well until the labor pains kicked into second gear. We've only seen him once since we got here."

Glancing at the wheelchair, Cass said, "I see you made another deal with the doctor."

"He thinks he's so smart," she said disgustedly.

"He said there couldn't be a safer place for me to be than a hospital. If I keel over, he said someone will just pick me up and shove me into a bed."

The waiting room began to fill up as several crew members of the Gypsy Fleet arrived. They couldn't stay long as they had charters scheduled, but they had all known Salem for years and had to stop by to hear whatever news was available.

Josslyn from the gallery came by, then some of Connie's relatives, bringing enough food to feed the entire floor. It became a party of sorts, somewhat subdued but gay and happy at the thought of a baby, Salem's baby, being born.

Cass couldn't help comparing this hospital visit with the others she had spent in emergency rooms, when she'd had to bring Myra in after the older woman had hurt herself during a drinking binge. Then she'd been alone to deal with the situation. This time there were a number of people to share a much happier event.

When Wyatt eventually returned, everyone stopped whatever they were doing and looked expectantly at him. He laughed and shook his head. "Nothing to report." Then he gestured to Cass. "Salem wants to see you."

"Me?" Cass croaked, stunned.

Smiling, he held out his hand to her. "Come on. I'll take you to her."

As she walked beside him, she said, "I thought only fathers were allowed in with the mothers."

He shrugged. "I guess this is a progressive hospital. Since you and I are considered family, the nurse isn't making a fuss. I imagine once Salem's in the final stages of labor and they take her into the birthing room, only John will be allowed to go with her."

"How's she doing?"

"Great. She's one tough cookie," he said with pride in his voice.

That didn't tell her much, but she took her cue from him. He held her hand securely without any sign of tension in his eyes. Stopping at one of the rooms, he reached over her head and pushed open the heavy door for her.

Inside, Salem was lying in a bed that had been cranked up enough for her to partially sit up. A number of ominous machines had been wheeled up beside the head of the bed, making all sorts of peculiar sounds. John was standing at one side, his hand clasping his wife's. He looked a little pale under his tan, and smiled wanly at Cass as she approached the bed.

Salem gave an exaggerated sigh of relief. "Thank you for coming, Cass. Wyatt, take John down for a cup of coffee, please." Before her husband could voice the protest she could see forming on his lips, she held up her free hand. "Ten minutes. That's all, darling. I've been lying here resting while you've been pacing and lurking around the bed. You need a break."

"Lurking?" John exploded. "I've never lurked in my life."

Giggling, Salem glanced at Wyatt. "See? The man needs a bit of R and R if he's going to make it through this."

John leaned over and kissed her. "All right. I'll be back in ten minutes. Don't you dare have this baby until I get back."

"I wouldn't think of it."

Salem waved them off, then collapsed against the bed as the door shut behind them. She gripped the bedrail with the hand John had been holding and clenched her teeth. Realizing what was happening, Cass took her other hand, wincing as Salem's small fingers tightened painfully.

When the contraction was over, Cass said quietly, "You're remarkable, Salem. You were having pains when you were shooing John out of here, weren't you?"

"If he'd known, he wouldn't have left. Neither would Wyatt if I hadn't asked him to take John for a cup of coffee. Both of them have been hovering over me. They're like two worrywarts—in stereo. Don't think I don't appreciate them. I love them, but John is almost a basket case. I want him to make it to the delivery room."

Cass chuckled. "At least you don't have to worry about Wyatt. I imagine he's glad he can skip that part."

Salem grinned. "I think you're right."

"You have ten minutes. Do you want to tell me why you wanted to see me before they come back?"

"Or before another one of these lovely contractions grabs me again." Still holding Cass's hand, she became serious. "Once the baby comes, I want you and Wyatt to take John back to Delta's. There's a bottle of champagne in the refrigerator that Connie's been keeping for me. Give him a couple of glasses and shove him into bed. I know him. He's going to be exhausted, but he'll be worrying and fretting even when it's over. He'll need family around him then."

"Salem . . ." Cass began, but didn't know what to say.

Salem didn't have that problem. "Don't give me any guff about you not being family. You're as much family as the rest of us. You're Delta's daughter and you're involved with Wyatt. That makes you family."

"I never said I—"

Salem's gaze shifted to what Cass was wearing. "Nice dress, Cass," she drawled. "Looks rather familiar. Do you usually wear the same outfit two days in a row?"

Cass started to laugh, until she felt Salem's fingers flex in her hand. Perspiration broke out on Salem's face as she fought her way through another bout of pain. When it was over, Cass took a damp cloth off the bedside table and wiped Salem's face. "Wyatt was right. You're one tough cookie."

Catching her breath, Salem grinned. "Speaking of cookies, does Wyatt eat them in bed?" Ignoring the choking sound Cass made, she went on, "I've often wondered, since Lord knows he munches on them everywhere else."

To get Salem's mind off the subject of Wyatt's habits in bed, Cass began to tell her about some of the incidents she'd encountered while tending bar.

Salem was in the middle of another contraction when the door opened and the two men returned to the labor room. Cass held on to Salem's hand, ignoring the pain of the other woman's fingernails digging into her flesh. Wiping Salem's pale face with the cloth, she kept talking through the contraction as though nothing untoward was happening. She finished the story as John and Wyatt approached the bed.

"I asked him to put his hands on the bar, palm down, and then set a full drink on the back of each of his hands. There wasn't a thing he could do without spilling either drink."

Gasping for breath, Salem stared at her wide-eyed. "What happened?"

"I called his wife. He was still sitting there with the drinks on his hands when she showed up. She took one and threw it on his lap, telling him to cool off. The other went into his face. Then she took him home."

Salem laughed. "I bet that's the last time he tried to feel up a waitress." Holding out her hand to her husband, she grinned. "See, I'm still here."

Wyatt stood beside Cass, his hand automatically resting on the small of her back. There was a curious glow of satisfaction in his eyes as he glanced from Salem to John. "We've been going at this all wrong, John. Instead of making comforting noises at her, we should have been telling her dirty jokes."

Salem's eyes lit up. "Do you know any?"

At exactly ten minutes after seven in the evening, Carrie Marie Canada finally made her entrance into the world. It was ironic that the one person who should have felt in need of rest was the only one who had any amount of energy left. From her hospital bed, Salem took one look at their faces and ordered them all to go home and get some rest. Including John.

Wyatt was in the process of turning Delta's

wheelchair around when he caught the look Salem gave Cass. Cass immediately put her arm through John's and began to lead him out of the room.

"Tell me again," she said, "how Carrie looked up at you and smiled when you held her for the first time."

Wyatt looked back at Salem. She winked at him and blew him a kiss. Suddenly he laughed. He couldn't help it. Even from a hospital bed, Salem Shepherd Canada was capable of managing things her own way. The fact that Salem had enlisted Cass's help in getting John home pleased him immensely.

When he and Delta entered the waiting room, he couldn't help noticing how Cass was doing the same thing—taking over—only in a quieter way. He wondered if she realized she was doing it. In the time between punching the button to summon the elevator and its arrival, she had everything under control. Connie was going to have a celebration dinner with some of her relatives. Her nephew, Clovis, would see that Delta got home safely. She and Wyatt would drive John back to Delta's, where John would call one of the charter captains, who would spread the word of the newest addition to the Gypsy Fleet crew.

Once at the house, Wyatt watched in fascination as she continued to subtly run the show. She handed him a bottle of champagne, instructing him to open it. Then after Delta had toasted the baby, Cass asked him to carry Delta back to her room, where the two of them settled the exhausted artist into her bed. Afterward Cass listened patiently as John sat at the kitchen table and gave a second-by-second account of the delivery for the third time, topping up his glass of champagne at various intervals.

Wyatt wondered if Cass even realized what was happening. She was fitting in, making a place for herself, even though she might not be aware of it. It was obvious Salem had asked her to ensure John got some rest, but she was taking on everything else all on her own, automatically, instinctively. For an independent woman, a loner, she was involved up to her pretty little neck in their lives, he mused.

He couldn't have been more pleased. He wanted her to know she was where she belonged, where people cared about her and she cared about them. Her actions that day didn't fool him into thinking everything was going to run smoothly from then on. He knew there were still problems ahead, but nothing that couldn't be solved with time. And love.

He was in love with her. There was no doubt in his mind about his feelings. Wondering how she felt about him, though, tied his guts in a knot.

He was stirred from his thoughts by John, who was frowning at the glass sitting on the table in front of Cass. "That's not fair. You keep pouring champagne into my glass, but you haven't touched yours."

Before Cass could respond, Wyatt said casually, "She'd rather have milk." Taking her glass, he tossed the contents into the sink on his way to the refrigerator. He poured milk into the glass and brought it back to the table, smoothly, effortlessly, as though it was perfectly normal to prefer milk over champagne.

Picking up his own glass, he lifted it high and made a toast. "To Carrie Marie Canada, who will undoubtedly run us all as ragged as her sweet mother does."

Then it was Wyatt's turn to take charge. John didn't object when Wyatt suggested he call his wife, then go to bed. After John left the kitchen, Wyatt took Cass's arm, brought her up out of her chair, and drew her with him to the back door.

Stopping at the door, he cupped her face in his hands, brushing his thumbs across the soft skin under her eyes. "Will you be able to get some sleep?"

She smiled through her disappointment that he was leaving. "I can almost guarantee it. It's been quite a day."

He stroked one thumb across her bottom lip, feeling the moisture against his skin. "And you didn't get much sleep last night," he said softly. Sighing, he added, "As much as I would like you to come back to the cottage with me, I know you need sleep. If you went with me, you wouldn't get any."

Cass couldn't hold back the shiver of awareness his words created, or the pictures in her mind that flared up as vividly as the desire simmering under her skin. She knew he was right, but she didn't have to like it.

Wyatt almost lost his good intentions when he felt her tremble. Lowering his head, he allowed himself one taste, one brief kiss before he left. It would have to last him until he saw her again.

They were both breathing raggedly when he lifted his head. "Will you spend tomorrow with me?" he asked. "We never did get a chance to go out into the Gulf. I could take you tomorrow if you'd like to go."

She reached up and clasped his bandaged hand. "Why don't we wait until you can go diving? I've been on a boat before, but I've never been diving. I would love to learn how."

"You got it. I happen to know a good diving instructor who would give you his undivided attention." He grinned. "In or out of the water. We'll go tomorrow. Everyone's gone to a lot of trouble so that we can spend the day together. We wouldn't want to disappoint them."

"What are you talking about?"

"John did some fancy maneuvering to get a boat free for our use."

"Why would he do that?"

"I imagine Delta asked him to. Why waste the opportunity? Go out with me tomorrow. I'd like to show you my underwater world."

"You still have stitches in your hand, Wyatt," she said soberly. "The salt water wouldn't do your injury any good."

"I'll wear a glove." He kissed her briefly again, then stepped back. He was dying by inches. It was small consolation to know he was doing the right thing by leaving her.

Concern still ate at Cass. She wanted to go diving with him and learn why he loved it so much, yet not at the cost of him hurting himself. But he was the expert, she considered. He should know what he could and could not do in the water.

Feeling the tension that emanated from him, she tried to lighten the mood. "Maybe I'll be lucky enough to find some buried treasure before I leave."

"Don't," he said harshly. She flinched at his raised voice. "I don't want to hear about your leaving, Cass. Not now." Not ever, he added silently. "And if it's treasure you want . . ." He reached into his shirt and drew the gold chain over his head, then draped it over hers. The medallion settled in the space just above the cleft of her breasts.

"Wyatt, no. You can't give me this. It means too much to you."

He cupped the back of her neck and drew her to him. "So do you, Cass," he murmured against her mouth.

There was a desperate, hungry quality to the way he took her mouth. Stunned by the emotion in his voice and the kiss, Cass leaned into him to take everything he offered her.

All too soon, he raised his head. Running a finger down her cheek, he said, "I'll see you tomorrow."

All she could do was nod in agreement, her fingers searching for the coin hanging from the chain around her neck.

Nine

Whether it was Wyatt's expert instruction or
Cass's natural ability, she soon learned how to
use the diving equipment properly. First Wyatt
took her to the small water tank in the building
near the marina where he had his diving school.
He wanted to make sure she could handle the
breathing apparatus in a controlled situation
before introducing her to the vagrancies of the
ocean, with its currents and underwater
attractions.

The diving school was a revelation to Cass.
Compared with Wyatt's less than tidy cottage, the
school was clean and very orderly. All the equipment was neatly arranged on shelves. Wetsuits
were hanging neatly on racks. Diving masks, fins,

and an assortment of other diving paraphernalia were available for sale in the small shop at the front of the building. Cass was impressed. As casual as Wyatt appeared about most things, the diving school was obviously something he took very seriously.

It also made her wonder how many more sides of him she would discover in the short time she had left on the island. The more she was with him, the deeper she fell into love with him, and the harder it was going to be to leave.

She stored up each smile, each touch, each word he said, tucking them away in her mind for the day those memories would be all she'd have. Wyatt had said he didn't want to hear about her leaving, so she didn't mention it, but it was on her mind every minute she spent with him.

Wyatt took her to a cove of one of the uninhabited islands of the Keys. It was a fairly safe area for her to have her first experience underwater, with enough attractions to keep her fascinated, yet nothing more dangerous than a strip of coral and some colorful tropical fish. He stayed beside her the whole time, pointing to various sea creatures and guiding her from one sight to another. The water glided over her skin like cool satin, and she was glad Wyatt hadn't insisted on her wearing one of the wetsuits he normally wore when he went diving. He'd explained they weren't going to be underwater long enough for her skin to become too chilled.

She was disappointed when he called a halt to the dive after thirty minutes. If it had been up to her, she would have stayed underwater until the sun went down.

"Why do we have to stop so soon?" she asked as he hauled her up onto the deck of the boat.

Wyatt smiled as he helped her off with her tank, pleased she had enjoyed herself. "You aren't used to the weight of the tank. Even though it feels light when you're underwater, your body is under more of a strain than you think. Plus, wearing fins when you aren't used to them can cause muscles in your legs to cramp up."

Picking up a towel, she began to rub off the drops of salt water clinging to her skin. "I can see why you love diving, Wyatt. It's incredible. Like entering another world."

He felt his body harden as he looked at her. The sun was glistening on her skin; the wind tousled her hair around her face. Her eyes glowed with the joy of her first attempt at diving. His gaze followed the trail the towel made, lingering on the expanses of silky skin revealed by the small strips of cloth she wore. His medallion lay against her chest.

He removed the rubber glove he'd worn on his injured hand and let it fall to the deck. It took only one step to bring him close to her. Taking the towel from her, he rubbed it over her stomach, her hips, down her curving thighs, smiling to himself when he heard her breathing quicken. Then he retraced the path he'd taken, slower and slower, his fingers caressing her through the rough fabric. When he stroked the towel over the soft swell of her breast, he heard her say his name and raised his gaze to hers.

Cass shuddered under the onslaught of the delicious hot sensations she was suddenly immersed in. In the water she'd never been in danger of drowning as badly as she was now. Drowning in a sea of sensuality, drawn down into a whirlpool of passion she'd never known existed until she'd been taken there by Wyatt.

She slid her hands over his damp chest. Her voice was husky as she ordered, "Drop the towel."

He smiled. "Why?"

"It's in the way."

His gaze fixed on her mouth. "Of what?"

"Of you touching me."

Releasing the towel, he let it fall unheeded on the deck. "Do you like me to touch you?"

"Yes." She brought her hands down over his rib cage to the waistband of his suit. His gaze locked with hers, heat stirring in the depths of his blue eyes. "Do you like it when I touch you?"

He closed his eyes as he felt her hand slide lower, lingering over the hard ridge under the slippery material of his suit. "I love your hands on me," he said, groaning. "Anywhere. Everywhere."

He gripped her arms to bring her to him, and she flowed against him. Hunger and need jolted through him, as hot and as searing as lightning the moment his mouth covered hers. One kiss became another, then another, and soon it wasn't enough.

The small part of Wyatt's mind that could still function was aware of the hot sun beating on them, as scalding as the desire pouring over him. Without relinquishing the feel of her tongue mating with his, he drew her under the canopy covering the wheelhouse. Stopping when he felt the captain's chair behind him, he swiveled it around and perched on the seat, positioning her so that she was standing between his legs.

He raised his head and looked down at her as he swept away her bikini, until the only thing she wore was his medallion. Then he brought her hands to the waistband of his suit, encouraging her to help him slide it off. When he was naked he gently, insistently, drew her thighs over his, and groaned when she lowered her body onto him and took him deep inside of her. Her hands clasping his shoulders, her breasts stroked his chest as she moved above him in a sensual dance that spun him into ecstasy. He cupped her hips to help her as their bodies thrust together, finally taking over completely when she tired.

The breeze off the ocean caressed their heated bodies, but they didn't feel anything except the flames of sensuality licking at their flesh, finally consuming them. Their cries of pleasure were carried off in the wind, joining the other forces of nature.

Wyatt buried his face in her neck to ride out the delicious aftershocks. The thought of never being able to have her again once she left the island made him tighten his hold on her. He suddenly froze as reality came crashing down on him. He swore under his breath.

Startled, Cass raised her head and looked at him. "What's wrong?"

With his hands at her waist, he helped her off him, then cupped her face between his hands and met her puzzled eyes. "I'm sorry, Cass. I know that's inadequate, but I—"

She stared at him, stricken. "You're sorry you made love to me?"

"No. Good Lord, no." He smoothed her damp

hair away from her face, his thumbs soothing and caressing her. "All I could think about was being inside you. I didn't protect you, Cass."

Considering her background and his, she should have been alarmed. So why wasn't she? Cass wondered as she thought about the possibility of being pregnant with Wyatt's child. It wasn't nearly as frightening as it should be under the circumstances. To have a child to love would make up for all the lonely years she'd endured without having anyone of her own. Wyatt's child. One thing she was positive of was she would never give her child away.

"It's all right," she said calmly, surprising him. "The chances of my conceiving from this one time are slim. And according to the wordy pamphlets in the doctor's office, this isn't the right point in my cycle."

Wyatt stared at her. She was taking this very well. Too well. "It only takes one time. If you are pregnant, you don't need to worry about facing it alone."

If that statement was his idea of reassuring her, Cass mused, it didn't hit the mark. He was willing to acknowledge his responsibility in the matter, but that was the only commitment he'd make.

"I can handle it," she murmured before turning away from him.

His gaze followed her as she picked up the bottom of her bikini, and his body tightened when she gracefully slipped it on. The woman was driving him crazy in more ways than sexually. If she thought he was going to let her handle a pregnancy alone, she was sadly mistaken. Nor was she going to leave the island when her two weeks were up.

His first impulse was to pull her into his arms and insist she marry him immediately, but he controlled it. Bending down, he picked up his swimming trunks instead and tugged them on. Tonight he would take her out to dinner, someplace where there was soft music and candlelight. Then he would take her back to the cottage and ask her to marry him. He wasn't much for making romantic gestures, but she deserved more than a hasty proposal on top of the warning about possibly being pregnant.

Suddenly eager to put his plans in motion, he turned back to the wheelhouse and started the engine. He pressed the button to winch up the anchor before pushing the throttle forward. Whistling under his breath, he began to formulate his scenario for the evening.

After tonight he wouldn't have to hear any more about her leaving the island and him.

Cass couldn't believe it. The blasted man was whistling. One minute he's telling her he might have gotten her pregnant, the next he's calmly piloting the boat and whistling as though he didn't have a care in the world. If she didn't love him so much, she could very easily hate him.

She was even more bewildered when he took her directly to Delta's house, driving faster than normal, as though he were in a hurry to dump her off.

At the back door he leaned down to kiss her lightly. "I'll be back at seven to pick you up."

"Why?" she asked with a hint of temper. "I thought the diving lesson was over."

"It is," he said, his smile broad, his eyes glittering with humor. "Tonight is something else altogether."

She watched as he strode purposefully to his Jeep and practically leaped inside. She tried to control her hurt at the thought that he was in such a hurry to get away from her. Her emotions had taken a real roller coaster ride that day, and she was having difficulty finding her balance now that he had pushed her off.

Connie's voice intruded into her worries. "There you are, child. I didn't expect you back this early. Where's Mr. Wyatt?"

Good question, Cass thought as she followed Connie into the kitchen. "He had other things to do. He'll be back later. Don't plan on us being here for dinner."

"Fine." Connie's dark gaze swept over Cass, taking in the windblown hair, the salt-coated skin, and the sadness in her eyes. "Didn't you enjoy the day on the water?"

"Very much." Knowing that the older woman's eyes were sharp enough to detect a gnat at twenty yards, Cass tried to hide her feelings from her. "I didn't realize how tiring diving can be. I think I'll go up to my room and shower off this salt water. Unless," she tacked on, "there's something you want me to help you with."

"I don't need any help, thank you, Miss Cassandra. But Miss Delta said she would like to see you. She has something important she wishes to discuss with you."

"I'll go see her as soon as I've had a shower," Cass said, hoping she sounded more enthusiastic than she felt.

"Perhaps it would be better if you waited until a little later. I believe she is resting now."

"Is she all right?" Cass asked with concern.

Smiling broadly, the housekeeper nodded. "She hasn't been this well in a long time. You have been good for her, child. She's just taking a rest. Nothing for you to worry about."

"I'll get started on cleaning up the studio, then."

As she climbed the stairs, Cass remembered she also had to call the clinic to see how Myra was doing. Her carefree moment in the sun was over. It was back to reality.

Feeling at least cleaner if not calmer after a shower, Cass tucked a black knit top into a pair of pleated khaki walking shorts. After obtaining some cleaning materials from Connie, she set out for the studio, relieved she had something to do to occupy her until Wyatt came at seven. Maybe she would be able to come up with some answers before she saw him.

Then again, maybe she wouldn't.

After tackling the dust and cobwebs, Cass needed another shower when she returned to the house thirty minutes before Wyatt was to arrive. She chose a white sarong-style linen skirt to wear with an emerald-green silk top, which had a scoop neck and short sleeves. She had a white linen jacket to take with her, although as warm as the day was, she might not need it. She thought it would be better to be prepared, considering she had no idea what Wyatt had planned for the evening.

She left her bedroom and a minute later entered Delta's room after tapping several times on the door. She stopped abruptly when she saw Delta wasn't in bed. Dressed in one of her safari outfits, the artist was sitting at a small desk set against one of the walls near the bed.

"Connie said you wanted to see me, Delta."

"Yes, dear. Come in and sit down." Tapping the legal-size pad in front of her, Delta said, "I've been jotting down a few things you'll need, and I wanted your input before I send Connie off to purchase everything."

Cass took the chair near the desk. She had no idea what Delta was talking about, but there were a few things she was going to have to make clear. She knew she was going to sound defensive, but it couldn't be helped. After the episode with Wyatt on the boat, she didn't want any more misunderstandings.

"I don't want you buying me anything, Delta. That's not why I came."

Chagrined, the older woman shook her head. "I'm sorry, Cassandra. As usual I'm jumping ahead without waiting for anyone to catch up. I've been so wrapped up in making the plans, I've forgotten to tell you what they were."

"What plans?" Cass asked with caution.

Delta's eyes were shining with enthusiasm as she turned to face Cass directly. "I was so pleased the other night when you came late to the dinner table because you'd been in the studio. It gave me a wonderful idea. I realized I have a chance to make up to you for all the years of neglect, by offering to pay your tuition at the art school I attended in Paris. I've made all the arrangements." If she heard Cass's sharp intake of air, she preferred to ignore it. "Myra will come here when she's released from the clinic. The change will be good for her. You will be free to pursue your art training without having to worry about her."

Feeling like a snowball in the path of an avalanche, Cass could only stare at Delta as the woman's words rolled over her. This was certainly a day for surprises, she thought aimlessly. And the day wasn't even over. There was something oddly tragic in the fact that she was being put in a situation similar to the one Delta had been in twenty-seven years ago. She was being offered an art education when she might be pregnant.

"Delta," she began hesitantly, trying to search for the right words so that she wouldn't hurt the older woman's feelings. The truth would have to do. "Painting doesn't mean the same to me as it does to you. It doesn't consume me with the same passion as it does you. I don't want to go away to Paris." She sprang out of the chair and began pacing the carpeted floor. "I don't even want to leave Key West. I'm sorry if that hurts you after all the plans you've made, but it's the truth."

Because her back was to Delta, she didn't see the gleam of satisfaction in the older woman's eyes. "Why don't you want to leave Key West?" Delta asked.

"It's complicated."

"Life usually is."

"Maybe I should just leave and go back to Biloxi," Cass said, giving voice to the thought that had been lingering in the back of her mind since the trip back from the cove.

"Running away never solved any problems, Cassandra," Delta said firmly. "I should know. I ran away from the responsibility of having a child and have had to pay the heavy price of not seeing you for most of your life."

Cass halted her pacing and turned to face her. "Why did you leave me with Myra, Delta? I'd really like to know."

Delta didn't answer immediately. Finally she said, "Have you ever had a desire for something you thought you would never have? Then suddenly, after it appears hopeless, your wish comes true? That's what happened to me. At the age of forty my husband was gone. He'd left me enough money to support myself in France while I studied art. I had this house, and Connie agreed to stay here to take care of it while I was gone. There was nothing to stop me from finally realizing my dream to become an artist. Except one thing."

"Me," Cass said flatly.

"I know how selfish I sound, Cassandra, to turn my back on my own child. It was selfish and something I've regretted all these years. At first you were to stay with Myra only while I was gone. When I came to New Orleans two years later, you seemed happy. And Myra didn't want to give you up. At the time she was making a good living and could give you a better home than I could until I got better established in the art world. I returned here to paint. Somehow the years were flying by and you were growing up just fine without me. I kept putting off telling you the truth until it was too late. But I never once stopped caring about you. Not one minute. If you believe anything, believe that."

"I didn't before," Cass said softly, "but I do now."

Delta gazed steadily at Cass. "It would give me great pleasure if you feel you could confide in me, Cassandra. I haven't been there for you in the past, but I'm here now."

Shaking her head, Cass began pacing again. "It isn't because I feel I can't confide in you." She returned to her chair and sank down onto it, as though the weight of the world was on her shoulders. "It's not easy to admit I've made a royal fool of myself."

"That usually means a man is involved. Men can make us feel like complete idiots when all the time they are the ones acting like jackasses." Delta paused as though weighing her words, then added, "What has Wyatt done to upset you?"

Cass smiled crookedly. "Not a lot gets past you, does it?"

"I'm an artist, Cassandra. I wouldn't be a very good one if I didn't see what was around me. I see the way Wyatt looks at you and the expression in your eyes when you say his name."

Cass didn't bother to deny how she felt about Wyatt. "It isn't so much what he's done, as much as it is what he hasn't said. He told me he doesn't want me to leave, but he doesn't give me a good enough reason to stay."

"So what are you planning to do?"

Suddenly Cass knew. Leaving her chair, she went over to Delta and knelt down in front of the older woman. Placing her hands over Delta's, she spoke calmly and sincerely. "I want you to know I appreciate the offer to send me to art school, Delta. I'm sorry if it disappoints you, but I really don't want my life centered on painting."

Delta's sharp eyes never left Cass's face. "What is it you do want?"

"Wyatt," she said frankly. "A home, children, the works."

Satisfaction gleamed in the artist's eyes. "Wyatt wouldn't leave the island, you know. Have you thought about that? Would you be happy staying here?"

"Yes." After a moment Cass asked, "Were you serious earlier about bringing Myra here?"

"Of course. I don't know why I didn't suggest it several years ago when I suspected Myra was having problems. I think it would do her good to come here, and I would like to have her here."

Cass nodded. "Good. I wouldn't abandon Myra. As for myself, when I worked at the gallery the other day, Josslyn said she could use some help, if not full-time, then at least part-time. I'm sure I could find some other job too." She smiled wryly. "I could always tend bar.

"Even if things don't work out with Wyatt, I'd still like to stay on the island. For the first time in my life I feel like I belong somewhere. The only reason I stayed in Biloxi was because of Myra. If she agrees to come here, then I don't have to leave for good."

Cass stayed with Delta for a few minutes more, then returned to her room to finish getting ready for Wyatt. Even though nothing had been settled between her and Wyatt, she felt at ease with her past and her surroundings, as though all the pieces of her life were finally fitting into the right places.

Glancing at her watch, she saw that she still had time before he was due to arrive. Rather than go downstairs, she sat on the window seat and stared out at the ocean in the distance, partially blocked by trees and the roofs of houses. A gentle breeze ruffled the curtains on either side of the open window, bringing the scent of flowers and salt air.

She had meant what she'd said to Delta. She did feel like she belonged here. It wasn't just the place but the people. She enjoyed spending time with Salem, was treated by Connie as though she'd always been there, and was able to understand Delta's earlier motives for leaving her. She had enjoyed the feeling of being needed the night Salem gave birth to the baby. It was a different, warmer feeling than the one of obligation she'd had for Myra for more years than she wanted to remember.

Even if her relationship with Wyatt didn't develop into what she wanted, she would still stay on the island. She brought her hand up to touch the medallion that lay between her breasts. As much as she hated the thought, she knew the day might come when she would have to return his medallion. Whether she was pregnant or not, she wouldn't be able to continue an affair indefinitely without a commitment from Wyatt. Especially if she was pregnant.

Her door opened abruptly, and she turned her head to see who it was. Wyatt, dressed in light-tan slacks and a tan-and-white-striped shirt, strode into the room and shut the door forcefully behind him.

"Is it true?" he asked.

"Is what true?" she asked without moving.

"I just came from Delta's room. She was on top

of the world. I found out why. She informed me she had offered to pay your way to Paris, complete with tuition to an art school."

"That's true. She did make that offer."

He stared at her for a long moment, as though he'd never seen her before. Finally, shoving his hands into the front pockets of his slacks, he said, "I see. For someone who protested about coming back to the island with me, it's turned out to be fairly profitable for you, hasn't it? Delta's taking over your care of Myra, you're getting a free trip to Paris with an education thrown in. One thing she didn't happen to mention was that you might be pregnant. Apparently you left that little tidbit out of the conversation."

With effort Cass hid her fierce hurt at his accusing tone of voice. "No," she said with forced calm, "I didn't mention the possibility to her."

"So when do you plan to leave?"

If he had sounded regretful instead of angry, she might have told him she wasn't leaving at all. "Are you anxious to get rid of me, Wyatt?"

Something explosive entered his blue eyes. Ignoring her question, he growled, "I don't believe this. Were you even going to discuss this with me, or were you just going to pack your bags and take off?"

"I was going to tell you about Delta's offer tonight."

"What about the possibility that you might be carrying my child? Were you planning on sending me a postcard in a couple of months, or were you going to handle it like you do everything else, no matter what the outcome is?" His voice hardened. "Let me warn you. No child of mine will be given away. If you are pregnant, you damn well better tell me."

"I'll let you know," she said quietly.

"Since you apparently came to the island to get whatever you could out of the situation, I guess I shouldn't complain that I was included, since I'm the one who twisted your arm to come. Well, it's been fun, Cass, but you'll have to leave me out from now on. I don't like being used, even by you."

"What did you want from me, Wyatt?" she asked, surprised that she could still talk through the tightness in her throat.

At the door he turned to look at her over his shoulder. "I guess you'll never know now, will you?"

After he had left, Cass continued staring at the door. Then she raised her chin. He might not be willing to fight to keep her there, but she was certainly going to fight for her right to stay.

Ten

Since she hadn't been able to sleep during the long night, Cass had used the time to repack her suitcase with some essentials she would need in Biloxi. The clothes she wasn't taking were hung up in the closet or tucked into the dresser drawers. The significance of leaving some of her belongings in the room didn't escape her. Unlike the feeling of trespassing when she first arrived, she now felt as though this was no longer Salem's room, but hers.

She waited until eight in the morning before phoning Salem at the hospital. Connie had mentioned that Salem and the baby would be going home sometime that day, and Cass asked Salem if she could stop by the hospital before John arrived. She could tell by Salem's voice that she was puzzled by the urgency of Cass's request, but Salem didn't ask any questions. She just told her John would be by around ten that morning.

Because she was pushed for time, Cass took a

cab to the hospital rather than walk. A few minutes later she strolled into Salem's room. Dressed in a flowing blue skirt and flower-print shirt, Salem was putting the last of her personal items into the small case on the bed.

"Hi," Salem said, her eyes gleaming with curiosity. "Did you see the baby?"

"No. I would love to see her, but I can't take the time right now. I'll see her when I get back."

Salem frowned. "Get back? Where are you going?"

"I'm going to Biloxi to make arrangements for Myra to come to Delta's after she gets out of the clinic. I'm also going to close up my apartment, which might take a couple of days, and quit my job. I'll give the company two-weeks' notice, so it will probably be a couple of weeks before I can return to the island."

"You're going to stay here permanently?" Salem asked, smiling broadly.

"If I can persuade Myra to come once she's released from the clinic."

Salem's smile disappeared suddenly. "Wait a minute. Something isn't quite right here. John said Wyatt came to the house last night and was in a mood to kick things. All John could get out of him were jumbled bits and pieces about Paris, artists, and something about candlelight and roses. When John tried to get him to sit down calmly and talk, Wyatt muttered about going diving for at least a week where all he had to contend with were sharks and barracudas." She tilted her head to one side. "It would make sense if he doesn't know you'll be coming back."

"He left last night before I had a chance to tell him."

Salem pursed her lips in a silent whistle. "It sounds like you had a slight disagreement."

"Something like that." In a few brief sentences Cass told Salem about how Wyatt had misinterpreted the offer Delta made to send Cass to Paris. "Obviously Delta neglected to tell him I had refused her generous offer."

"It sounds like her. Delta has the patience of a saint when it comes to painting, but she tends to push a bit when she thinks other things are going a little too slow. When John and I were having problems, she told him I was taking a job in California. It worked. He kidnapped me that night and took me to one of the uninhabited islands and told me I wasn't going anywhere and that I was going to marry him "

"Well, if her plan was to push Wyatt, it didn't work out that way this time." Reaching into her shoulder bag, Cass removed an envelope and handed it to Salem. "Would you see that Wyatt gets this?"

Salem frowned as she felt something bulky inside the envelope. "What is it?"

"A check he gave me in Biloxi to cover my expenses while I was in Key West. I never did plan on cashing it, but he didn't know that." She paused. "And his medallion is also inside."

"The fact that he gave you this medallion should tell you something, Cass," Salem said seriously. "It's his most prized possession."

"That's why he should have it back."

"Don't you think you should return it to him in person?"

Cass shook her head, then hugged the younger woman. "I've got to run. I've got a taxi waiting for me outside and just enough time to catch my plane. I'll see you when I get back."

"Are you sure this is the way you want to do this? If Wyatt knew what you planned to do, he would go with you and help with all the arrangements."

Cass smiled faintly. "I can handle it."

Salem watched as Cass turned and walked out of the room. For a moment she stared down at the envelope in her hand, then carefully laid it in her suitcase.

Two days later Wyatt parked his Jeep at John and Salem's house. He really wasn't in the mood to be around people just yet, even John and Salem, but he'd finally been worn down by John's persistent badgering about coming for dinner. He hadn't seen the baby since the day she was born, and innocent Carrie Marie had been used as blackmail to get Wyatt to come to the house.

He was still feeling raw and frustrated, not exactly the best company. But he wouldn't be seeing just anyone. John and Salem would put up with him no matter how foul his mood.

They were out back enjoying the fresh air while John did his duty at the grill. Salem was setting the picnic table when Wyatt slid open the French doors and stepped outside. The baby was in a wicker bassinet near the table. His heart twisted painfully at the domestic scene. Only a short time ago he had envisioned a similar scene featuring himself and Cass.

He accepted a beer from John and walked over to the bassinet to stare down at his honorary niece. Salem slid her arm through his.

"She's been asking for you."

Wyatt smiled. "I don't know much about babies, Salem, but I doubt if they know how to talk at five days old."

"Some things don't have to be put into words. Feelings can be read in a person's eyes no matter how old they are. Like yours, for instance."

"Salem," he warned. "Let it go."

"I can't do that. Do you remember the time at the orphanage I got a splinter in my foot when I stepped on a board?"

He didn't know what a splinter had to do with anything, but he went along with her. "I also remember I practically had to sit on you in order to remove it. You've always been a stubborn cuss, brat. That hasn't changed."

She dismissed his comments on her character with a gesture of her hand and got back to the point she was trying to make. "You saw I was hurting and insisted on doing something about it. Right now you're hurting, and we want to help you. We're friends, you know. We're family. Family should stick together, not shut each other out."

He put his arm around her and hugged her. "I know. I'm sorry. I had a few things to work out, and I had to do it myself."

"And have you?" she asked quietly.

"Not even close," he admitted. He looked down at her. "Why do I have the feeling you already know why I've been sulking? Did you talk to Delta?"

She shook her head. "No. Cass."

He set down the bottle of beer and shoved his hands in the front pockets of his jeans. Just hearing her name tightened the knot in his stomach. "How is she?"

"I don't know. She's gone."

His head jerked up. "What do you mean, she's gone? Delta said the next term didn't start until September."

Salem took his arm and drew him away from the bassinet. Straddling the picnic bench, she sat down and tugged on his arm until he sat beside her. "Think carefully. Did Delta say Cass would be enrolling in the fall, or just that the next term started then?"

Wyatt frowned. "I don't remember. What difference does it make?"

John brought over a platter of steaks and set them down on the table. "It makes a big difference," he said. "Delta is great at setting up situations to suit her purposes. You were sitting at the dinner table a couple of years ago when she said she was going to sell the house and move into an apartment. She claimed the house would be too big for just her and Connie once Salem left to take a job in California. She'd had no intention of selling the house, though. She only said that to shake me up. I couldn't let Salem leave, and Delta knew it."

Wyatt tried to remember exactly what Delta had said about Cass and Paris. At the time all he could think of was that Delta had offered to send Cass to art school. As he went over the older woman's exact words in his mind, he couldn't recall a single word about Cass actually accepting.

When he'd confronted Cass in her room, she hadn't said she was going to accept Delta's offer, just that the offer had been made. Now he wondered if her answers had been evasive because of the way he'd asked the questions.

He shut his eyes as he also remembered what else he'd said to Cass and the hurt expression on her face. Opening his eyes again, he stared at Salem. "Are you telling me Cass isn't going to Paris?"

Salem nodded, smiling with smug satisfaction. "That's what I'm telling you."

"Then where is she? You just said she was gone."

"She's in Biloxi, but only for a couple of weeks. She's giving notice at her job and clearing out her apartment."

This seemed to be the night for revelations, Wyatt thought, feeling life returning to his heart, which had felt dead the last couple of days. "She's coming back."

He'd made a statement, not asked a question, but Salem answered, "Absolutely. Frankly I don't envy her tackling all the arrangements on her own, but I guess she can handle it. At least she said she could."

The familiar phrase made Wyatt smile, something he hadn't done for three days. "She's good at that."

"Apparently she's had to be," John murmured. He looked long and hard at Wyatt. "I've never known you to give up when there was something you wanted. Why start now?"

Wyatt's mouth twisted into a self-mocking smile.

"I've been trying to think of what I could offer her that would be better than a trip to Paris."

"How about yourself?" John suggested. "She evidently thinks staying here is better than going to Paris, since she turned Delta down." He paused for a moment, then added, "So are you just going to sit around and wait for her to come back, or are you going after her?"

Wyatt stood up. "I'm going after her. This time I'm going to keep my mouth shut and let her tell me what she's going to do, instead of jumping down her throat with accusations."

Salem nodded in complete agreement. "That sounds like a good idea to me. You might as well sit down and eat one of these delicious steaks John has gone to the trouble to cook. While we eat, we can put our heads together and come up with a way to get you out of the hot water you dove into headfirst." She slid her hand into the pocket of her denim skirt and withdrew an envelope. "Here. I'm supposed to give this to you."

Puzzled, Wyatt slid his finger under the flap and opened the envelope. His medallion fell into the palm of his hand. He didn't slip it over his head. Instead he shoved it into his pocket. Even though he'd worn it for years, he no longer considered it his. The person it belonged to now was in Biloxi.

He was about to crumple up the envelope when he felt something else in it. Thinking it might be a note from Cass, he unfolded the paper and recognized the blank check he'd given her in Biloxi.

Sitting back down, he said, "Do you think Terry

Braddock would feel like taking a trip across the Gulf in his seaplane tonight?"

Cass was having a strange dream. The bed under her was undulating like a raft on a rough sea, then the motion abruptly stopped. She felt something solid and warm against her hip, but as she attempted to roll away from it, she was stopped.

Feeling as though she were being pulled out of a deep dark sea, she opened her eyes and blinked several times. The small boudoir lamp on her dresser was on, giving off just enough light for her to see who was sitting beside her on the bed.

Was it possible to dream while you were awake? she wondered. Maybe she was still dreaming. In case she wasn't, she whispered, "Wyatt?"

"Who else would be sitting on your bed at six o'clock in the morning?"

She blinked again. He sounded amused, familiar, and real. His hand was warm and firm on her hip, where he'd placed it to keep her from rolling away from him. Pulling herself up into a sitting position, she leaned back against the headboard and stared at him.

"You'll have to give me a minute," she said drowsily, pushing her tousled hair out of her eyes. "I didn't expect you."

"Take all the time you want. I'm not going anywhere."

The last dregs of sleep were gone and hope was taking its place. "Why are you here?"

"You forgot two things when you left the island. I decided to bring them to you."

"What did I forget?"

He smiled. "This." Reaching into his pocket, he withdrew something and held it out to her.

The gold chain glittered in the light. His medallion. "That isn't mine. It belongs to you."

"Not anymore." When she didn't take it from him, he slipped it over her head. Satisfaction glittered in his eyes as he looked at the medallion resting against the white fabric of her nightgown.

She had to be still dreaming, Cass thought. It was the only explanation. "What was the other thing I forgot?"

His gaze locked with hers. "Me."

"You weren't all that anxious to be with me the last time we talked. What changed your mind?"

He needed to touch her, and settled for taking her small hand in his. "I didn't change my mind about wanting you with me. That's why I overreacted when Delta told me she had made arrangements for you to go to Paris. Having a trans-Atlantic affair wasn't part of my plans."

She drew her hand out of his warm clasp. "Having an affair of any kind isn't part of my plans."

"What are your plans? I'll listen this time, Cass," he said seriously. "I didn't last time and you left the island without talking to me. That was my fault, and I don't want that ever to happen again. Tell me what you want."

She lifted her chin defensively. "I'm coming back to the island."

The knot of tension in his stomach began to loosen. Even though Salem had told him Cass would be coming back, he hadn't actually believed it until he heard her say it herself. "For how long?"

She lifted her hand to the medallion and fingered the coin. It was odd how it gave her confidence and hope. "For however long it takes to make you realize you can't live without me."

"Cass." He groaned as he lifted her into his arms. Holding her tightly, he spoke against her neck. "I've known that for a long time."

Drawing back, he looked down at her, then lowered his head to kiss her. His mouth was tender at first, soothing her and himself with the slow, intimate slide of his tongue against hers. Then it changed. They had been apart four long days and nights, with misunderstandings making that time seem like forever.

Breaking away from her mouth, he buried his lips in her throat. "I'm sorry, Cass. I've been acting like a spoiled brat who threw a tantrum because he wasn't getting his way. I had been so wrapped up with the plans I'd made for that night that when I heard Delta talk about sending you to Paris, I went a little crazy."

Cass wrapped her arms around his neck to hold him. It seemed like a miracle that he was there with her. "What were your plans?"

Raising his head, he met her gaze. "I'd spent all afternoon setting up a romantic dinner at my cottage. Candles, roses, soft music, the whole works. I was going to wine and dine you, then propose."

She nearly choked, but caught her breath as she stared at him. "Propose?"

He smiled. "Propose as in 'man and wife, forever and ever.' "

"Why didn't you say anything about proposing when you came to my room that night? All you did was rant and rave about the blasted trip to Paris."

He brought his hands up to cup her face, then kissed her briefly. "Maybe I wasn't sure you would think living with a part owner of a charter-boat business would be suitable compensation for missing out on a trip to Paris."

"You're an idiot," she said bluntly.

"I know. Believe me, I've called myself a hell of a lot worse things than that the last four days. Can you forgive me?"

"It depends."

"On what? Whatever it is, I'll do it, say it, promise it. As long as I don't lose you again."

Dropping her arms, she slipped off the bed and walked over to the dresser. Near her jewelry box was a small votive candle she kept on hand for when the electricity went off during storms. She lit it, then turned on the portable radio she had planned to pack that day. Opening up a drawer, she withdrew a white silk gardenia that had come from one of the packages of Filmer's Fancy Fudge. Carrying it back with her, she stood in front of him.

"We have candlelight, soft music, and a flower. Say it."

"Cassandra, will you marry me?"

"Yes."

The gardenia dropped to the floor as Wyatt swept her up in his arms and lowered her to the bed. His hand slid over her, finding the hem of her nightgown and drawing it up to her waist. "I love you. I was so afraid I'd lost you."

Her fingers went to his belt buckle. "I was too."

Caressing the slight curve of her stomach, he

said huskily, "Do you think you'll mind living with a pigheaded, stubborn, arrogant male?"

She smiled as she slowly unfastened his jeans. "I can handle it."

THE EDITOR'S CORNER

Each month we have LOVESWEPTs that dazzle . . . that warm the heart or bring laughter and the occasional tear—all of them sensual and full of love, of course. Seldom, however, are all six books literally sizzling with so much fiery passion and tumultuous romance as next month's.

First, a love story sure to blaze in your memory is remarkable Billie Green's **STARBRIGHT,** LOVESWEPT #456. Imagine a powerful man with midnight-blue eyes and a former model who has as much heart and soul as she does beauty. He is brilliant lawyer Garrick Fane, a man with a secret. She is Elise Adler Bright, vulnerable and feisty, who believes Garrick has betrayed her. When a terrifying accident hurls them together, they have one last chance to explore their fierce physical love . . . and the desperate problems each has tried to hide. As time runs out for them, they must recapture the true love they'd once believed was theirs—or lose it forever. Fireworks sparked with humor. A sizzler, indeed.

Prepare to soar when you read LOVESWEPT #457, **PASSION'S FLIGHT,** by talented Terry Lawrence. Sensual, sensual, sensual is this story of a legendary dancer and notorious seducer known throughout the world as "Stash." He finds the woman he can love faithfully for a lifetime in Mariah Heath. Mariah is also a dancer and one Stash admires tremendously for her grace and fierce emotionality. But he is haunted by a past that closes him to enduring love—and Mariah must struggle to break through her own vulnerabilities to teach her incredible lover that forever can be theirs. This is a romance that's as unforgettable as it is delectable.

As steamy as the bayou, as exciting as Bourbon Street in New Orleans, **THE RESTLESS HEART**, LOVESWEPT #458, by gifted Tami Hoag, is sure to win your heart. Tami has really given us a gift in the hero she's created for this romance. What a wickedly handsome, mischievous, and sexy Cajun Remy Doucet is! And how he woos heroine Danielle Hamilton. From diapering babies to kissing a lady senseless, Remy is masterful. But a lie and a shadow stand between him and Danielle . . . and only when a dangerous misunderstanding parts them can they find truth and the love they deserve. Reading not to be missed!

Guaranteed to start a real conflagration in your imagination is extraordinary Sandra Chastain's **FIREBRAND**, LOVESWEPT #459. Cade McCall wasn't the kind of man to answer an ad as mysterious as Rusty Wilder's—but he'd never needed a job so badly. When he met the green-eyed rancher whose wild red hair echoed her spirit, he fell hard. Rusty found Cade too handsome, too irresistible to become the partner she needed. Consumed by the flames of desire they generated, only searing romance could follow . . . but each feared their love might turn to ashes if he or she couldn't tame the other. Silk and denim . . . fire and ice. A LOVESWEPT that couldn't have been better titled—**FIREBRAND**.

Delightful Janet Evanovich outdoes herself with **THE ROCKY ROAD TO ROMANCE**, LOVESWEPT #460, which sparkles with fiery fun. In the midst of a wild and woolly romantic chase between Steve Crow and Daisy Adams, you should be prepared to meet an old and fascinating friend—that quirky Elsie Hawkins. This is Elsie's fourth appearance in Janet's LOVESWEPTS. All of us have come to look forward to where she'll turn up next . . . and just how she'll affect the outcome of a stalled romance. Elsie won't disappoint you as she works her wondrous ways on the smoldering romance of Steve and Daisy. A real winner!

Absolutely breathtaking! A daring love story not to be missed! Those were just a couple of the remarks heard in the office from those who read **TABOO**, LOVESWEPT #461, by Olivia Rupprecht. Cammie Walker had been adopted by Grant Kennedy's family when her family died in a car crash. She grew up with great brotherly love for Grant. Then, one night when Cammie came home to visit, she saw Grant as she'd never seen him before. Her desire for him was overwhelming . . . unbearably so. And Grant soon confessed he'd been passionately in love with her for years. But Cammie was terrified of their love . . . and terrified of how it might affect her adopted parents. **TABOO** is one of the most emotionally touching and stunningly sensual romances of the year.

And do make sure you look for the three books next month in Bantam's fabulous imprint, FANFARE . . . the very best in women's popular fiction. It's a spectacular FANFARE month with **SCANDAL** by Amanda Quick, **STAR-CROSSED LOVERS** by Kay Hooper, and **HEAVEN SENT** by newcomer Pamela Morsi.

Enjoy!

Sincerely,

Carolyn Nichols

Carolyn Nichols,
Publisher,
LOVESWEPT
Bantam Books
666 Fifth Avenue
New York, NY 10103

THE LATEST IN BOOKS
AND AUDIO CASSETTES

Paperbacks

☐	28671	**NOBODY'S FAULT** Nancy Holmes	$5.95
☐	28412	**A SEASON OF SWANS** Celeste De Blasis	$5.95
☐	28354	**SEDUCTION** Amanda Quick	$4.50
☐	28594	**SURRENDER** Amanda Quick	$4.50
☐	28435	**WORLD OF DIFFERENCE** Leonia Blair	$5.95
☐	28416	**RIGHTFULLY MINE** Doris Mortman	$5.95
☐	27032	**FIRST BORN** Doris Mortman	$4.95
☐	27283	**BRAZEN VIRTUE** Nora Roberts	$4.50
☐	27891	**PEOPLE LIKE US** Dominick Dunne	$4.95
☐	27260	**WILD SWAN** Celeste De Blasis	$5.95
☐	25692	**SWAN'S CHANCE** Celeste De Blasis	$5.95
☐	27790	**A WOMAN OF SUBSTANCE** Barbara Taylor Bradford	$5.95

Audio

☐ **SEPTEMBER** by Rosamunde Pilcher
Performance by Lynn Redgrave
180 Mins. Double Cassette   45241-X $15.95

☐ **THE SHELL SEEKERS** by Rosamunde Pilcher
Performance by Lynn Redgrave
180 Mins. Double Cassette   48183-9 $14.95

☐ **COLD SASSY TREE** by Olive Ann Burns
Performance by Richard Thomas
180 Mins. Double Cassette   45166-9 $14.95

☐ **NOBODY'S FAULT** by Nancy Holmes
Performance by Geraldine James
180 Mins. Double Cassette   45250-9 $14.95

- -

Bantam Books, Dept. FBS, 414 East Golf Road, Des Plaines, IL 60016

Please send me the items I have checked above. I am enclosing $_____
(please add $2.50 to cover postage and handling). Send check or money order,
no cash or C.O.D.s please. (Tape offer good in USA only.)

Mr/Ms _____

Address _____

City/State _____ Zip _____

Please allow four to six weeks for delivery.
Prices and availability subject to change without notice.

FBS–1/91

60 Minutes to a Better, More Beautiful You!

Now it's easier than ever to awaken your sensuality, stay slim forever—even make yourself irresistible. With Bantam's bestselling subliminal audio tapes, you're only 60 minutes away from a better, more beautiful you!

__	45004-2	**Slim Forever**	$8.95
__	45035-2	**Stop Smoking Forever**	$8.95
__	45022-0	**Positively Change Your Life**	$8.95
__	45041-7	**Stress Free Forever**	$8.95
__	45106-5	**Get a Good Night's Sleep**	$7.95
__	45094-8	**Improve Your Concentration**	$7.95
__	45172-3	**Develop A Perfect Memory**	$8.95